Beware of false prophets who come to you in sheep's clothing,
but inwardly they are ravenous wolves.
Matthew 7:15–20

❧ ❧

BRIDES OF EDEN

❧ ❧

BRIDES OF EDEN

A true story imagined

LINDA CREW

HARPERCOLLINS*PUBLISHERS*

Library of Congress
Cataloging-in-Publication Data
Crew, Linda
  Brides of Eden / by Linda Crew.
    p.   cm.
  Summary: In this story based on true events,
sixteen-year-old Eva and her female friends become
obsessed with a charismatic young man who comes
to Corvallis, Oregon, in 1903, claiming to be a
Christian prophet.
  ISBN 0-06-028750-0 — ISBN 0-06-028751-9
(lib. bdg.)
  [1. Cults—Fiction.   2. Fanaticism—Fiction.
3. Faith—Fiction.   4. Christian life—Fiction.
5. Corvallis (Or.)—History—Fiction.]   I. Title.
PZ7.C86815 Br 2001   00-40904
[Fic]—dc21
            Typography by Alison Donalty
         1 3 5 7 9 10 8 6 4 2
            ❖ First Edition

This is a true story.

The events are documented in the historical record, and the characters are real people.

Their personalities and relationships, however, are in large part the author's invention.

The resulting novel, *Brides of Eden*, is respectfully dedicated to the memory of Eva Mae Hurt.

BRIDES OF EDEN

THE CORVALLIS TIMES

March 28, 1903

LOCAL LORE.

— B. J. Evers has treated his house, barn, and other outbuildings to a neat coat of paint.

— A dressed hog at Homer Lilly's shop attracted some attention Friday forenoon on account of its size. It was two years old, fatted by William Leadbetter, and weighed four hundred pounds dressed.

— Night Officer Overlander will not expect any whining from the fellows who hereafter get arrested for riding bicycles about the streets and walks after night without lamps. He wishes to have it known that he intends to enforce the law on this subject.

— Juanita Lorena, the two-year-old child of Mr. and Mrs. P. L. Withrow, was buried Thursday afternoon in Odd Fellows cemetery. The little one's death was caused from pneumonia, after a hard struggle with the formidable malady.

— Miss Vieve Cecil entertained a number of friends at her home Saturday evening. Hearts was the chief amusement, and the evening was very pleasantly spent. Dainty refreshments were served.

CHAPTER ONE

*H*ow could such a thing happen in Corvallis, of all places? That's what they'd be asking themselves for years to come. As if nine Christian churches must certainly be enough to save a mere two thousand souls from such doings. As if tidy picket fences alone could keep the female population contentedly at home. As if lacing us tightly enough in our corsets must surely guarantee protection from all evil.

Can you imagine? they would ask one another with a shudder, clearly entertained by their own titillating speculations. *How could all those girls have done that?*

But for our family there has never been the slightest amusement in it, and we would forever be haunted by a more painfully personal question: How could such a thing happen to *us*?

In our defense, I can say only that nothing seemed so terribly strange in the beginning. There were no portents of doom, no angel at the gate warning us of the perils that lay beyond.

It began, I suppose, with our family's involvement in the Salvation Army. I'd been taken along to meetings for years, and I'd always tried to be the best lassie I could. That's what they called us girls—lassies.

My father, Orlando Victor Hurt, declined to join, although he seemed to think well enough of the organization's aim of social justice. I don't know how seriously he took it, though. He only brought it up when teasing us with the currently popular song "Salvation Lassie of Mine." Every time we came down the stairs in those dreary uniforms, he'd start singing it: *They say it's in heaven that all angels dwell, but I've come to learn they're on earth just as well. . . ."*

This never failed to make me smile, but it didn't amuse my older sister Maud, who always stopped him at the first phrase with one dark look. Religion was a solemn business with her, and she would brook no disrespect concerning the Salvation Army. Why, when she was fourteen and newly a member, she even insisted on wearing the drab regulation suit for her eighth-grade graduation photograph. And her classmates were all in white-lace flounces!

Personally I would have chosen the white lace too, but I did admire Maud's convictions. She seemed so sure of everything, whereas I, six years younger, was sure of nothing. I tried to be good, honestly, and I looked to her constantly for reassurance I was succeeding. What I got more often than not, though, was a blue-eyes-to-heaven look that told me I had succeeded only in once again sorely trying her patience.

It was Maud's approval I craved more than anyone else's, I think, the year I was twelve and competing in a nationwide contest to see who could sell the most copies of the Salvation Army newspaper, *The War Cry*. Everyone was saying I would certainly win, judging from the tallies, but a boy back East came from behind in the final days and I only placed second. Papa said that was still very good, but after the local buildup, I felt rather let down, and Maud rubbed it in by commenting that it was too easy for me anyway. "Eva just smiles," she said, "and they buy." The guitar sent as the second prize annoyed me somehow, arriving with the assumption, it seemed, that not only would I know how to play it, which I didn't, but also that I would immediately join the army's street corner band. Honestly, if I was too shy to stand shaking a tambourine, what made anyone think I'd agree to fumble in public with a guitar?

Disillusioned with the Salvation Army after that, I grew curious about the other churches in town.

"Why can't we go to a regular church?" I remember asking. "Couldn't we go to the Presbyterian or the Episcopal?" Secretly I preferred the chime of a church bell to the boom of the Salvation Army's big bass drum.

"Eva." Maud shook her head, despairing of me. "Trying to be a good Christian is more than a nice little social outing. Are you sure you don't want to go to Good Samaritan Episcopal just so you can look at all the fancy hats?"

"No!" I said, but not without blushing at the hint of truth in this.

"Or maybe it's just that you like those angel statues on the chimneys."

"I do not," I said. "I mean, I do, but . . ." Oh, there was no living up to Maud for being a good Christian.

People still talked about what an amazing child she'd been for taking to the gospel. Only eight years old when she started getting up at revival meetings, imploring sinners to come forward and save themselves. No one could get over it, this little dark-haired girl, so terribly earnest. And now, at twenty-two, she was forever marching off to nurse some family through their illnesses, even typhoid, never worrying for herself, always declaring it no more than her simple Christian duty.

Lately she'd taken to chiding me for what she called my worldliness, which seemed a bit unfair. As if anyone could be worldly in Corvallis! Why, when the handful of students at Oregon Agricultural College went home for the summer, the unpaved streets were so deserted, the newspaper joked of dogs dozing all day in the middle, undisturbed. And that wasn't far from the truth!

But Maud simply wouldn't leave off about a fancy five-dollar petticoat I'd bought down at Kline's. She'd been hoping Papa would forbid it. Instead, since he's the manager of the grocery department there, he was able to arrange a discount.

"What is he thinking?" she said when she found out. "Spoiling you this way."

"I'm not spoiled!" I protested. To me it only seemed the way of things. Maud was closer to Mama, and if Papa, perhaps, favored me, was that my fault?

I was sixteen when the trouble began. My school days were past, my future was a blank page. Further education did not particularly appeal to me; neither did the pursuit of the two main occupations open to us girls — teaching or nursing. Maud was engaged to James Berry, and my older brother Frank was working as a shipping clerk in town, courting Mollie Sandell, who'd come down from Seattle with the Salvation Army.

I imagined I too would be courted and married sooner or later, but so far I hadn't had any sweethearts. So that spring I was simply waiting, wondering what might happen next in my life.

What happened was a man named Franz Edmund Creffield.

Hoping to make our little town his mission, he had come to Corvallis as a member of the Salvation Army.

From the first moment I laid eyes upon Mr. Creffield at an army meeting, I knew he was a definite cut above any man I'd ever met. He had an appealing halo of blond curls — none of the greasy, pomaded locks of the other men in town. His pale and piercing eyes were set the slightest bit on the close side, so that when he took my hand that first time and looked straight at me, I felt absolutely riveted.

"Eva Mae," he said upon being told my name. "I'm so pleased to meet you."

"This is the little girl who won the prize for selling so many copies of *The War Cry*," I heard someone say, and I blushed at the reminder of my childish triumph. *Little soldier boomer*, the newspaper article had called me. How embarrassing.

"Ah," he said. "A young woman of selfless devotion. I admire that."

Now I blushed all the hotter, suddenly happy to claim myself a boomer, if it meant his approval. And he called me a young woman! Still, I knew I wasn't one bit selfless, and I hoped he wouldn't hear how few copies I'd actually sold recently. Oh, I should have kept it up better! As I stood there, dazzled by this handsome man, exquisitely conscious of my hand still in his, all these thoughts tumbled over themselves in my mind until I could hardly manage to stammer some vague reply. The way he was looking at me, giving me his undivided attention! I'd never felt singled out like this before, and I must say I quite liked it.

The other girls were drawn to him too. Before long we were all quoting him. It was "Mr. Creffield says this," and "Oh, no, Mr. Creffield doesn't agree with that."

He had a fiery style of oratory that enlivened things considerably, and he could not testify on the street corner without it becoming a sermon that kept every listener spellbound. He spoke up at meetings too, and we all began to look forward to his interesting interruptions.

Naturally the other Salvation Army officers didn't appreciate a newcomer taking over leadership of the group, but as Maud said, let *them* speak with the power of Mr. Creffield if they wanted our attention.

We started out good girls, you see, and if at our meetings there was a handsome, well-spoken young man, likewise concerned with the improvement of his spiritual life, well, who was to find anything amiss in that? Would we have better earned the respect of the community by loitering about the doors of the local taverns, waiting for the young ne'er-do-wells to spill out at closing?

Our family lived just over the bridge south of Corvallis, where the Mary's River runs into the Willamette. Separated from town by the Mary's and the expanse of flood-plain pasture known as the flats, we were still close enough to hear the whistles of the riverboats announcing their arrivals at the town landing and to feel the rumble of passing trains. From our front porch we could see, about a mile distant, the clock tower of the county courthouse jutting above the big leaf maples.

One day one of the Salvation Army lassies appeared at our back door, flushed and excited.

"Sophie!" was all I managed before she rushed past

me into the kitchen where Maud, Mama, and I had been sitting around the stove, mending.

"Mr. Creffield," she announced, "has left the Salvation Army!"

"But that's terrible," I said, stricken at the thought of meetings without him. Why then was Sophie absolutely bouncing on her toes with excitement?

"No, you see, it's a good thing," she said, "because he's going to start a new church!"

Maud frowned. "What do the officers say?"

"Who cares?" Sophie said. "No one's going to want to stay with the Salvation Army now."

Maud thought a moment. "No," she said matter-of-factly. "I suppose they won't. *I* certainly won't."

"Maud," I said, surprised. She'd been such a staunch supporter of the army. And beyond that, the whole idea of a new church struck me as strange. To me, churches were institutions already set in place. "Can a person do that?" I said. "Just . . . make a church?"

"Mr. Creffield could," Sophie declared. "And we have to! We can't lose him! Really, how often does a person get a chance for Bible study with such a learned man? I've learned more from Mr. Creffield in two months than I have in all my time up at the college." She paused, devoting to him a moment of reverent silence. Then she looked at us expectantly. "Well, are you coming?"

"Now?" Mama said.

"Why not?" Sophie beamed. "What better time? We're having the first meeting right in our own parlor."

Church in a parlor? It seemed a bit odd, but heaven knows I was only too glad to ball up the frayed lace curtain I had repaired far too many times already and stuff it in the basket.

"Oh, and I should tell you," Sophie said as we stripped off our aprons and hastily repinned our hair. "This is important. He wants us to call him Joshua now. Joshua the Second."

Joshua. I liked the sound of that. And what a bold thing for a man to do — simply cast off an old name for a new and better one.

I felt bold, too, tripping across the Mary's River bridge behind the others. How daring, this abandonment of housework, this going off to hear preaching in the middle of a weekday afternoon!

$\mathcal{S}$ophie Hartley's elegant house was perfect for our meetings; we had it all to ourselves. Her father was hardly ever home since he had an important position at the Bohemia Mines down in Cottage Grove, and her brother was a student up at the college.

In this well-appointed home, our first meetings, I'm sure, would have looked to an outsider like any other sedate gathering in polite society.

Until Joshua started preaching, that is.

"There are times when we know," he began in low tones one afternoon, "that we've traveled all our lives simply for the purpose of arriving at a certain very important place at a very important time."

He paused, scanning the faces of the two dozen of us, his eyes taking in each individually.

"I, myself," he went on, "have made it my life's journey to be here, in this place, at this time, to bring you this message."

I glanced across the parlor at Attie Bray, my cousin. She'd told me once that when Joshua talked this way, about coming long distances, she felt certain he was referring specifically to her. After all, she was the one who'd traveled to be here, having come to Corvallis for schooling superior to what was available on the sparsely settled coast. When I pointed out that this was seven or eight years ago, she just said it only showed how complicated it could be, time and distance-wise, when God was working His purpose out.

Now she gazed at Joshua with the purest adoration, her expression giving her angular face a lovely glow. She looked almost pretty.

"I'm here to ask you to come away," Joshua said. "Come away from the world and all its evils. Will you do that?"

"Yes," we murmured.

"Will you do that for me?"

"Yes, Joshua, yes!"

"'Enter ye in at the straight gate,'" he read from Matthew. "'For wide is the gate and broad is the way, that leadeth to destruction, and many there be which go in thereat. Because straight is the gate, and narrow is the way, which leadeth unto life, and few there be that find it. . . .'"

Such power in that voice! It filled the room, filled our ears, filled our hearts. I stared, transfixed, as the phrases rolled over and around me like ocean waves, sweeping me off once more.

"How does he do it?" I asked Maud as we drifted home, still in the weakened, dreamlike state his preaching produced. Before a meeting I might feel ordinary and calm, thinking surely my mind exaggerated in remembering the fierce intensity of the previous day's sermon. Yet as soon as I entered the Hartleys' parlor and once more submitted myself to Joshua's penetrating stare and booming voice, I would again be overcome.

"He does it," Maud said, "by the grace of God. By the power of the Holy Spirit."

And truly, what else could it be?

One night at dinner Maud made a shocking announcement.

"I should let you all know," she said calmly, "that I've broken off my engagement to James Berry."

"What?" Papa said as around the table forks stopped halfway to mouths. "Why'd you go and do that?" He'd always made it plain he thought Mr. Berry, who owned the bicycle shop, a fine match for Maud.

"Joshua doesn't think I should marry him," Maud said.

"Joshua!" Papa exclaimed. "Since when does he tell people whom to marry and whom not to marry?"

"He didn't," Maud said primly. "He only made me see what's right. I should have seen it sooner myself. Mr. Berry doesn't have the spiritual depth I need in a husband."

Poor Papa. He looked so bewildered. And I can't say I blamed him. Maud wasn't getting any younger, and it wasn't as if she'd been fending off marriage proposals right and left. On the other hand, if she didn't want to marry the man, why should she? To be honest,

I'd never liked James Berry much myself. Oh, he was handsome enough. But there was something in his manner that put me on guard.

"I thought you said he'd been coming to your meetings," Papa said, still looking for a better explanation.

Maud sniffed. "What does that prove? Maybe he was only trying to please me. I need a man who wants to please God."

Papa frowned. "Eva Mae, did you know about this?"

I blinked, astonished. I *never* knew what Maud planned to do next.

"Sarah?" he said, looking next at Mama, who gave a little shrug and suddenly decided she had to fetch more rolls from the kitchen.

"Well," Papa said. "Well. This Mr. Creffield seems to hold a fair amount of influence, doesn't he?"

No one responded. We certainly couldn't deny it. And as it turned out, Maud's was only the first of many dramatic decisions made at Joshua's behest. The next was Sophie Hartley's. One day when we arrived early for services, Sophie told Maud and me that she was quitting college.

"The place is full of evil," she declared.

"What sort of evil?" I asked, wide eyed.

"Just . . . " She shuddered. "Evil. If I thought there was the slightest chance of bringing any light to that darkness, I'd have stayed, but it was no use. I mean, I went right into the office of the president of the college and offered to pray for him. He seemed agreeable. He even brought in two professors and persuaded them to kneel on the floor with me. And I prayed so fervently! They seemed impressed."

"What did you pray for?" I asked.

"Oh, that God would shine His spirit on them and help them do more for the spiritual welfare of all the students. But when I told Joshua about it, he was furious. He says there's no hope for them. They're defiled. All learning is the work of the devil, and I was debasing myself to even try to persuade them. So, I'm never going back there."

"But what does your father say?" I asked. "Weren't you almost ready to graduate?"

"That's the truly frightening part! I believe Joshua saved me just in time. I went right home and took a pair of scissors to that graduation dress Mama and I've been making."

I winced. "The white one with the cutwork?"

"Yes!"

I confess to a certain dismay. I had stood right there at Sophie's machine on several occasions, admiring all the fine lace insertions and edgings going into that gown.

"And the wonderful part is," Sophie said, "I've never felt better about anything in my life. Mama too. We threw it onto the burn pile in the yard and it was . . . well, it was thrilling. We looked at each other and we *knew*. We knew we were doing the right thing."

"Of course you were," Maud said, her eyes shining, seizing Sophie's hands. "This is truly a gift from God."

I stood there, looking on, feeling shut out somehow. Maud had always called Sophie shallow and frowned at her fashionable clothes; now she was giving her a look of such love and approval, the two of them lit up with this moment of sharing. I wanted that spirit to touch me too.

Then, in April, came a day that particularly sticks in my mind.

Joshua's sermon followed one of his favorite themes.

"'But they that will be rich fall into temptation and a snare,'" he roared, "'and into many foolish lusts, which drown men in destruction and perdition.

"'For the love of money is the root of all evil: which while some coveted after, they have erred from the faith, and pierced themselves through with many arrows.

"'But thou, O man of God, flee these things; and follow after righteousness!'"

He closed the Bible and stared straight at us. "If you believe this," he said, "if you believe in *me,* then I need your commitment. I need your help to bring the Kingdom of God here to earth. I need you to give up your worldly goods and turn them into the power that will save souls!"

We were nodding, swaying with this, calling, "Yes, yes, we will!"

"If you have money, give it to God. If you have

possessions or a business that can be turned *into* money, then turn it into money and give it to God!"

We were clapping and chanting. It made so much sense. It sounded so right.

After the meeting Mama started for home, but I stayed behind with Maud and another of our cousins, Esther Mitchell, the three of us lingering on the board-walk in front of the Hartleys', hoping we'd catch another glimpse of Joshua. Maybe we could even walk with him to his boardinghouse, as we sometimes did, on the excuse of asking clarification of some obscure Bible passage.

As we watched the front door for Joshua, Maud's ex-fiancé, James Berry, came out.

"Looks like that'll be it for me," he said, taking the steps with an almost jaunty air.

Maud made a point of turning away, gazing up into the blooming branches of an apple tree.

Esther frowned. "You're leaving the Holy Disciples?" Joshua changed the name of our group with fair frequency, and this was the latest of them.

"Well, I never considered myself an official member, you know."

"I thought Joshua said you'd made him a gift of money," Esther said.

I glanced at Maud. I'd heard this too. In fact, I suspected it was Maud who'd put him up to it when they were still engaged.

"Not a gift," Mr. Berry said. "A loan. Now he's

asking me to give him a note marked paid to it. And you heard what he said at the end there. All members have to give up their businesses? Turn their assets over to him?"

"Not to him," Esther said. "To God. 'Lay not up for yourselves treasures upon earth, where moth and rust doth corrupt.'"

Mr. Berry shoved his hands in his pockets and regarded her with a little smirk. "You know, Miss Mitchell, I've always thought you were far too pretty to be so prim."

We gasped at his impertinence. Flirting with Esther so soon after a broken engagement! And right in front of Maud! Well, too bad. I was confident he'd find what most of the other young men in town had already discovered: Esther didn't flirt. Everyone agreed she was the prettiest girl in Corvallis, but she was as cool and unapproachable as the snow queen in the fairy tale.

"I'd like to see you smile sometime," Mr. Berry was saying to her. "I'd like to hear you say something that wasn't out of the Bible."

Esther narrowed her eyes. "I'm perfectly capable, Mr. Berry, of discussing Joshua's teachings in my own words. He's only confirming what it says in the Bible many times."

Mr. Berry looked amused at this. "The Bible says I ought to give up my bicycle shop? I must have missed that verse. Does the Bible have any advice on how a man might make a respectable living?"

Esther regarded him coldly. "The Lord will provide."

"'Consider the lilies of the field, how they grow,'" Maud added. "'They toil not, neither do they spin.'"

"How convenient!" Mr. Berry laughed. "Since you all seem so happy to spend your time *not* toiling. And then, none of you has to worry about any assets to turn over. Yes, indeed. This looks to me like a fine plan on his part for making sure he's got nobody but you girls following him."

"We have men for members," I insisted, eager for a chance to defend Joshua like the other two, glad for a comment that wouldn't put my inferior knowledge of scripture to the test. "What about Sophie's fiancé, Lee Campbell? And my brother Frank?"

Mr. Berry looked at me as if I were an ignorant child. "Oh, certainly. And I'm sure your brother's involvement has nothing to do with Miss Mollie Sandell."

I blushed, flustered. True, Frank was smitten with Mollie, who'd been a captain in the Salvation Army but was now a Holy Disciple. When she left to follow Joshua, so had Frank.

Maud came to my rescue.

"Not everyone, James, sees everything in the basest possible terms, as you always do. Some of us are true believers. And just because the men can't come as often as they'd like doesn't mean they're any less sincere."

"Well, fine for them." Clearly the conversation was

beginning to bore him. "As for me, I have no intention of giving up my bicycle business. In fact, I plan to expand. I'm going to start selling autos!" He lifted his hat. "Good day, ladies." He mounted his bicycle and pedaled off along the unpaved street.

"There goes one lost soul," Esther said as we watched him lean and swoop around the corner.

I nodded, filled with admiration for the way Esther had spoken up with such authority. How did she manage it?

Perhaps she'd earned this confidence by being on her own more. Like me, she was the youngest in her family, but while I still had two parents to love and guide me, she'd lost her mother to typhoid fever when she was only seven years old. After that her father quit Newberg and returned to Illinois, leaving his children to shift for themselves.

From the day she first stepped off the train in Corvallis, Esther had turned heads with her graceful figure and luxurious blond hair. "Who *is* that?" people kept asking, and Maud and I were always ridiculously quick to claim her as a cousin. Well, she was—almost. Nell, her older sister, with whom she lived, was married to our uncle, Bert Starr.

Even now, years after her first appearance in town, Esther was still the object of the town's ardent, if distant admiration. In our group, we all deferred to her— even Maud, which, perversely perhaps, bothered me a good deal. Why did my sister always have to be so dismissive of me and then embrace this girl, who was my own age, as her bosom friend? Yet I could hardly complain when I was so taken with Esther myself.

Quite simply, I was dazzled by the blazing power of Esther Mitchell's beauty. I hung on her every word. I can't say I exactly *listened* to all of them, though, for while she was quoting Joshua or Jesus, I'd often be marveling at her amazing combination of dark eyes and flaxen hair, which she wore, like everyone else, twisted into a knot at the back of her head. Hers was prettier, though, somehow, with the variegated gold strands and those little tendrils that curled so charmingly around her face. I was forever wishing my own hair, once almost as light as hers, had not darkened in recent years to what I considered a rather dull brown.

Now when I recall that particular day and how we lingered in front of the Hartley house, it's not so much Joshua I think of, or Mr. Berry quitting the group. It's Esther I remember, and the light of the spring sunshine playing in her crowning glory of hair. I remember how the apple blossoms were dropping petals in drifts all around us, and the way I stood there gazing at her, smiling, but secretly nursing a case of gnawing envy.

CHAPTER THREE

Since our male members—including my brother
Frank—were finding it more and more difficult to daily
take leave of their various occupations, our afternoon
Bible study sessions did come to consist, as Mr. Berry
predicted, almost entirely of women.

"I believe I like it this way," Mama told Papa at the
dinner table.

"Well, yes, I think it's fine," Papa said, helping himself to a second serving of roast beef. "Sarah, another
wonderful dinner, my dear. Do you know, with the
meals you put on our table, I've often thought we could
have anyone in town to dinner and be proud. Why, we
could even have Mr. Kline's family!"

"Sure," Frank said, "if you weren't so scared of
him."

"What! I'm not scared of him. The man's my boss. I
respect him, that's all. I certainly have no trouble
speaking up to him. On these Bible meetings, for ex-
ample, just today he asked didn't I think it a bit odd, the

group being almost all female. And I simply said, 'Not a bit. We've always relied on our womenfolk to bear the standard, shall we say, for our spiritual lives.'"

And why is that? I thought as he reached to give Mama's hand a little pat and then motioned me to pass him the green beans. Why *were* there always more women than men in church—*any* church?

"Having mostly women in the group just seems more wholesome somehow," Mama continued. "I mean, for the girls. I'm sure it's much easier for them to concentrate on spiritual matters when they aren't worrying about impressing a churchful of young men."

Papa smiled fondly at me and I made my eyes big and innocent for him, hoping Maud wouldn't report how she'd caught me surreptitiously pinching my cheeks to bring up a pretty blush before climbing the Hartleys' porch steps.

"Well, I certainly don't want to encourage my girls to use church as a place to show themselves off," Papa said. "But I did think Maud—"

Mama cut her eyes at him. A warning. He coughed, choking off the rest of his remark.

"Maud *what*?" my sister demanded.

Papa colored, unwilling, or perhaps afraid to go on the way Maud was glaring at him. It was no secret he was disappointed in her broken engagement and worried about her matrimonial prospects. He told me once he thought her a trifle severe concerning religion, adding this wasn't usually the first thing a man looked for in a wife. He wished she were a little more yielding, he said. Sweeter—like me.

I have to admit, I enjoyed being his favorite, even if listening to such talk did make me feel a bit guilty.

"How much do you all really know about this Mr. Creffield's background?" Papa asked now.

"You mean Joshua," Maud corrected him.

Papa merely cleared his throat, unwilling, apparently, to speak Joshua's name. "There seem to be quite a few different stories going around town. That he's from a wealthy, well-educated Swedish family. That he'd been training for the priesthood. That he ran away from a dirt-poor farm family in Idaho."

None of these stories sounded right to me. I couldn't picture Joshua coming from any sort of family. I imagined him simply appearing from the clouds, as in some Bible illustration.

"I've even heard it said," Papa went on, "that he's an army deserter."

"I don't think any of us much cares," Frank said. "We're all more interested in the future than the past. You should be too, Pop."

"What! I'm interested in the future! Why, no one's more interested in the future than I am. Anyone will tell you that. How do you think I got elected Republican representative? Just ask your cousin Attie. 'Uncle Vic,' she said to me, 'Uncle Vic, you're the most forward-thinking man I know.'"

Maud and Frank glanced at each other, making plain they wished to heaven Attie had never made that remark, so often had they been forced to hear her quoted. But Attie was quite sincere. She always said she wished her mother, our mother's sister, had married a well-educated and enlightened man like Papa, for she couldn't abide her own father's rough ways.

"I'm more than willing," Papa continued, "to discuss *your* future, Frank, as you know. But then, you're not interested in my ideas on that subject."

"Pop," Frank said patiently. "We don't mean the future regarding my career. Or the city's future, the new sewers, or if we'll ever pave the streets."

"Well now, that sewer thing—the committee I was on—"

"Pop, we're talking about a bigger future. We're talking about the future of our souls."

The word hung there, less welcome to Papa, it seemed, than a black-clad mourner at a gay summer gathering.

"Our souls," he repeated.

"That's right, Pop. And we're concerned about yours."

"Well, don't be." Papa yanked his napkin from his collar band and pushed back from the table. "If any of you has anything pleasant or practical to discuss, I'll be in the parlor with the newspaper."

I made an impatient face at Frank as Papa left. Our father would join Joshua's church in good time, I thought, if Frank's arguing didn't serve to set him stubbornly against it. Sometimes it seemed to me Frank almost enjoyed taking the opposite side in any debate with Papa.

After I'd helped with the dishes, I went into the parlor, sat down at the piano, and began to play. I wasn't very good, not like Esther, who played all the hymns at our meetings. But Papa liked my playing well enough, and as the swells of "The Last Rose of Summer" crescendoed, I heard him sigh.

"Lovely, Eva," he said when I finished. "You always know how to make your poor old papa feel better, don't you?"

I spun on the stool and gave him my sweetest smile.

Now does that sound like such a crime? It was to hear Maud tell it. That night when I went to bed, she was lying in wait for me.

"Why are you forever trying to appease him, Eva? It's pathetic, the way you always scurry out to play that same old song for him."

"It's the only one I know!" I cried, which was true. Because my talents were so limited, I tended to concentrate my practicing on one piece at a time.

"That's not the point," Maud said. "With you it's always 'Oh, Papa, this,' or 'Whatever you think, Papa, that.' All he has to do is look cross, and I know in an

instant you'll be offering to fetch him a dish of ice cream
or somesuch."

Well, I wanted things to be nice around our house,
with Papa in a pleasant mood. If eating ice cream with
him helped, I was not averse to that. Why did she think
this such a huge transgression on my part?

Soon our growing numbers—thirty-five now—made
a meeting place bigger than Sophie's house essential.
So Joshua secured the use of the dilapidated old
Territorial Meeting Hall down on Main Street. With its
boarded-up windows and ramshackle air, it was hardly
in great demand by other groups, but it was fine for us.
What did we need with fine woodwork and stained
glass? Joshua decreed we would hold our ever more
rousing gatherings there at night.

In no time these nightly meetings became the talk
of the town. And the talk wasn't kindly.

When Maud and I came down Main Street, we were
no longer greeted with the open friendliness to which we
were accustomed. Instead, people whispered behind
their hands to their companions. As we passed, they
either nodded coolly, looking down their noses, or forced
a false and belated cheer. It was entirely new for me, this
feeling of being mocked, and I did not care for it one bit.

At Kline's grocery counter one Saturday, I met
with Mabel Allen, a former classmate. She was wearing
a crisply ironed shirtwaist and the most cunning straw

hat. I was about to exclaim over its charming trim of pert red cherries when she practically pounced on me.

"Well, Eva," she said. "I hear you're one of those Creffield people now."

A lady standing nearby gave me a cool looking over, sniffed, and turned away. I blushed, desperately hoping my father wouldn't appear at his office door. He was proud of our family's standing in the community; if he found out people were sneering at us, there'd surely be renewed argument at our house.

"So it's true?" Mabel persisted when I didn't answer.

I lifted my chin. "Yes, I'm a follower. So is my family." I glanced toward my father's office. "Well, mostly."

She wrinkled her nose. "But why? All that hollering. We can hear you clear over at our house, you know."

"It's just our form of worship," I said quietly, aware of the clerk listening even as he rang up my purchases.

Mabel's little pink mouth pinched up tighter than the drawstring closing of her coin purse. "Mighty strange, I'd say."

My cheeks flamed. But why should I feel embarrassed? I hadn't done anything wrong.

"You should have seen the look on her face," I told Maud later, slamming the fresh tin of baking powder on our wooden counter at home.

"This is the way it's going to be, Eva Mae. You'll have to get used to it. The ungodly have always scorned those of faith."

"But I always felt . . . that people *liked* me." I tied on my apron.

"Well of course they like you. *Everyone* likes you. So what?" She opened the kitchen bin and started scooping flour into her mixing bowl. "There isn't a true Christian in this town outside of our group. Why would you want to be friends with them?"

"You think that's true? No real Christians?"

"Well, look at them! You see how they march off to church every Sunday, all dressed up. But just let someone start preaching the true word, that they should give up their fancy things, and look how fast they fumble to find a way around it! They want to call themselves Christians without making any of the sacrifices."

Still, I thought as I mixed up a batch of bread dough, this didn't change the fact that I missed my friends.

"I had to tell Pearl I couldn't go maying with her this year because we had a meeting," I complained. "And I heard Hazel had a tea and I wasn't even invited! It's starting to seem like I don't have any friends at all anymore."

"Oh, fiddle, Eva. You have us. What your old friends call friendship is nothing compared to what we have. Why, we're bound together in our faith tighter than anything they could ever imagine. Remember that."

I nodded, but without great conviction.

"Besides, your old friends were all a bit silly, don't you think?"

I looked at her through my eyelashes. "That's what you used to say about Sophie."

"Well, you see? People can change. That's what the grace of God is all about."

She didn't have to say another word. We both knew what she thought — that I was the one who needed to work on changing.

I suppose she was right. I wanted to improve myself. I was tired of Maud always treating me like I wasn't quite good enough. And actually, I was beginning to *want* to be at the meetings all the time, because only there could I be joyously free of all these doubts. Under the spell of Joshua's magic, I felt as one with the others, one with the universe. I was part of something extraordinary, and, as Maud said, it was something my old friends could never understand.

"Every heart here," Joshua said from the meeting hall pulpit one night, "is beating with the love that passeth human understanding."

"Yes," we replied fervently. "Yes! Yes!"

"Join me in the earthly garden," he cried. "There we will shut out everything we've known before and make a new life. A life of holiness and purity. We must give ourselves to God, give up whatever has held us back, embrace God, embrace the joy of perfect obedience!"

"Yes! Oh, yes!"

Soon, as always, his individual words were lost in the swelling cadences, but our eyes remained riveted to his, and his meaning shot straight into our hearts. Now his voice was like thunder and his skin seemed to glow like Moses when he came down from the mountain.

"Give all to God!" he kept crying. "Give up your sins and the Lord will have victory tonight!"

"The Lord will have victory tonight!" At first we chanted softly, but slowly we built it to a powerful crescendo. We swayed, eyes closed now, our very spirits longing to separate from our bodies. We were going on a journey together. All of us, and I couldn't have stayed behind for the world. "The Lord will have victory tonight! The Lord will have victory tonight!" As one we rose then sank to our knees, pounding on the benches to raise a roar, all the time chanting, "The Lord will have victory tonight!" until the words lost all meaning but miraculously became the purer for it. A breathing in of the spirit, in and out, until I felt a tingling going through me and I fell to the floor with the others. Such a crying and a wailing, and all our private anguishes emptying from us, rushing forth, like creeks into a river, and all the rivers to the ocean. The window glass vibrated with the stomping of the floor and the pounding of the benches, like breakers on the shore, and the holy power of Joshua filled that room to where it seemed the very walls would surely crash into splinters at his command.

CHAPTER FOUR

*W*hen you get the fire," Joshua began his preaching one night, "you bring consternation wherever you go! Peace? No! There will be no peace when you make your appearance!"

"No peace!" we echoed.

"We are ablaze!" he cried. "We are baptized with fire! We're aflame with the Holy Spirit and we're too hot for the people of this miserable town."

A murmur of agreement ran round. Our neighbors disdained us quite openly now. And the curiosity! Police officers even had to be posted outside the hall to keep boisterous youths from disrupting our services.

"Instead of fighting sin, they're fighting us," Joshua went on. "They're lodging official complaints. And why? Because they cannot stand our light shining upon them, exposing their weaknesses, their compromises with the wickedness of the world.

"We are too loud, they're saying, when we cry out to the Lord!" Joshua let go a laugh, inviting us to join him in this mocking of the outsiders, the ungodly. "Can you imagine? Too loud for the Lord!"

When his face lit up that way, you forgot about the townspeople. You wished someone would say something to ensure that this glorious look continued. You wished it could be you.

When we quieted down, Joshua continued. "It makes me wonder, frankly, why the sinners are taking so much interest in our services."

His piercing gaze aimed at the back of the room. We all turned. Two men leaning against the back wall stood up, embarrassed. Grinning sheepishly, they ducked out.

"Now I have prayed on this," Joshua went on. "I have prayed all last night and all this day, and God has given me an answer. We will remove ourselves to a place I've found away from town—an island in the river."

The gathering would be like a regular revival meeting, he told us, but since the island campground was five miles out of town, it would be a waste to bother with buggies forever going back and forth. We would just camp there. We would stay all summer!

On the day before we left for the island, Papa lingered in the kitchen doorway as we put together a camping kit.

"It's beyond me," he said cheerfully, "why people enjoy these revival meetings. Sitting on a hard bench on a hot day, being threatened with damnation . . . but if that's what suits you . . ." And then while we debated which pots would be best for cooking over an open fire, he kept trying to distract us with jokes about hellfire and brimstone.

"Oh, Victor, stop," Mama said, finally losing patience. "I do wish you'd take all this more seriously."

Maud latched the lid of a wicker basket and looked up. "I don't know why you're not coming with us. I'm sure Mr. Kline would give you some time off."

"Yes, Papa, do come," I said halfheartedly, secretly hoping he wouldn't change his mind. True, his lack of faith concerned me, but I looked forward to a respite from our household's conflict on the subject. I longed for the tranquillity of being surrounded by none but believers.

Papa just laughed, though. "Oh, now, don't you all start with that again. And look here." His arm swept the kitchen. "What am I to do for my suppers? Are you leaving me a single pot?"

I will never forget the excitement of our departure day, the loading of our hired wagon. Had Grandmother Elizabeth felt like this, helping ready their covered wagons to cross the plains? We were always being reminded of our mother's proud pioneer heritage and how Grandma had been just fourteen when she made that trek back in the olden days. Now I felt we, like Grandma and the rest of her family, were pioneers, starting out on a glorious adventure, a new life.

Smith Island was no dot of land in the middle of the wide Willamette; rather it was a small wooded parcel bounded by two narrow forks of the river, wedged against a larger island, which was the setting of Mr. Kiger's peach orchard. The water in the surrounding sloughs dropped low enough in the summer to give easy access. At a certain fording spot, we were able to splash straight through in our wagon.

Once everyone had arrived, Joshua arranged with a professional photographer to make a group portrait to commemorate the founding of the camp. Our wicker chairs were pulled into a semicircle and we gathered, the twenty-one of us old enough to be counted official members. My own family was seemingly Joshua's inner circle. Maud and Mama sat on either side of him, Frank and his sweetheart, Mollie, right behind. They steered me to a seat next to Maud.

Just as the photographer's lifted trowel flashed, I thought of something: This was the exact arrangement in which we'd been seated for our Hurt family portrait, the one hanging above the mantel in a gilt frame. The only difference was, in Papa's place, we now had Joshua.

At first the gathering seemed like one lovely picnic. The full bloom of summer was upon us, with blue skies, lush green grass, and trees and flowers of every sort. When the pleasant breezes passed, the tall fir trees sighed, and the delicate scent of wild roses wafted around us.

To me, it was almost like a family reunion, we had so many relatives with us. There was Aunt Nell—Esther's sister—who was married to my mother's youngest brother, Bert Starr. Being only twenty-four, she seemed to me more like an older cousin than an aunt. Watching her stroll through the grove with her babies, I thought she looked like the sort of tall, handsome woman on whom sculptors modeled statues personifying lofty ideals of liberty, freedom, or peace.

With her was Aunt Hattie, who was married to Mama's *next*-to-youngest brother, Clarence Starr. Nell had brought her two little girls, and Hattie had a passel of boys. I did enjoy this riot of small cousins!

But my favorite cousin was still Attie. She'd grown up on her family's dairy ranch on the coast, and to me she was always like a blast of fresh wind off the ocean. She loved life out of doors, and now, on the island, she was in her element.

"Come on," she'd say to me, "let's catch some fish." We'd sit with our feet in the river and wait for dinner to swim by. The best part was, if we caught any, she knew how to clean them too.

Although it rained but little in the Willamette Valley during the summer, we built small arbors of boughs to sleep in, just in case. One was large enough for all of us to fit inside, completely hidden from the eyes of the annoyingly bold and curious townspeople whom we'd occasionally see spying on us from across the slough.

Among them was James Berry, who rode his bicycle out several times and even waded across to visit.

"I think he's still fond of you, Maud," I told her after his third appearance.

"Rubbish," she replied. "He's just like most poor sinners—what he can't have, he wants all the more. Believe me, it hasn't the least thing to do with true affection."

In a private spot on the island's far side, we bathed in the river and spread our laundered clothing on lines strung between trees.

We ate whatever came to hand, taking pride in our lack of planning, the deliberate absence of any regimen concerning meal preparation. I don't remember ever being hungry though, for as Joshua promised, God seemed to provide. Or perhaps I should say Mr. Kiger provided, for our diet leaned heavily toward the peaches collected in nighttime raids across the shallows into his orchard.

"But, Maud, what about the Commandments?" I had asked when Joshua first instructed us to help ourselves to the peaches. "Isn't that stealing?"

Maud narrowed her blue eyes at me. "Do you want to go ask Joshua that question?"

"No!"

"I didn't think so."

"But—"

"Eva Mae. How can Mr. Kiger think he owns the fruits of God's earth? Besides, would Joshua tell us to do something that was wrong?"

I was quick to shake my head no, although in truth, I wasn't entirely convinced.

But this was a small thing, and for the most part, I had no qualms about our way of life, which was proving delightful.

Joshua even issued a directive that we return to simpler, less restrictive clothing, and Cora Hartley and Aunt Hattie brought cotton goods and patterns for us to sew the old-fashioned, Mother Hubbard–style gowns he prescribed. Instead of whalebone corsets and dresses that weighed us down with layers of heavy pleatings and ruffles, we would now wear plain smocks of calico gathered at the neck with a drawstring.

What a sight we were that afternoon in the meadow when we finished our smock dresses and put them on for the first time! I pulled mine on over my head. Next, inside the little calico tent it formed, I unbuttoned and removed my shirtwaist. Then, I plucked loose the lacings of my corset and pushed it down over my hips to drop at my ankles.

"So much for this horrid thing!" I cried, and, laughing, kicked it into the blooming clover. How fine it felt to breathe so deeply.

And how it warmed me when Maud beamed with approval and promptly followed suit.

Soon we were all abandoning our corsets and letting down our hair. Maud looked gorgeous with her thick dark tresses tumbling over her shoulders and down her back. I'd never seen her like that, smiling and laughing, her cheeks pink.

Next we flung away our shoes. I loved the feel of the damp earth as I wriggled my bare toes deep into the grass, the way the warm breeze billowed my newly finished gown around my body. There was something so simple about it, so pure. I felt free. I felt newborn.

Of course there was more to our days than cavorting like children. Joshua prescribed many hours of prayer and the singing of hymns, but these rituals only made us feel more lit up with love and life, and our faces were constantly aglow with the joy of worship as we danced and raised our voices to the starry heavens. I had always regarded my singing voice as unremarkable, but, joining with the others in thrilling harmonies, I felt as if I had become a member of an angel choir.

> *"Blest be the tie that binds our hearts in Christian love;*
> *The fellowship of kindred minds is like to that above."*

In the center of all this was the sun around which we revolved—Joshua. He could not but step outside his private shelter without us gathering. If he found a seat on a stump, we surrounded him, edging to sit closer, vying to be the one at his very feet, there to gaze up at his face. More often than not, Maud and Esther were accorded this honor, but I sometimes managed to press close enough to feel I too had a special place in his heart. There I would sit, drinking in his words, hoping fervently all the while his hand would drop to my shoulder.

"You," he would say to us. "You, sitting here at this moment, are the light of the world. Do you know that?"

Brimming with joy, we would look around at each other. We felt so priviledged to be part of a group chosen, as Joshua kept promising, for a pivotal role in the destiny of the world itself.

Even when we left the formal meetings, much of our talk was of him: "Joshua says this. . . . " "Joshua forbids us to do that. . . ."

Everyone seemed to feel as I did, that Joshua was something for which she had been waiting, unknowingly, all her life.

"It's as if I'd been starving," Maud said, "and now he's given me a banquet."

To hear him speak was to step into a boat that was gliding down a shining river. Listening, you were pulled ever onward, mesmerized by the fluidity of his images and the wondrous pictures his words raised in your mind—the fountain of living waters, the rapture of angels, the power of God as He held our world in His mighty hands.

In Joshua's sermons I heard put into words things I had always sensed but never expressed. The virtue of simplicity. The importance of staying close to nature in order to be close to the One who made it all.

I learned new things too. The grace that comes with being free of all doubt, the comfort of releasing

one's mind from the tortures of excessive and unnecessary thought. Why fret? Why struggle to make sense of
difficult concepts? We had only to turn to the Bible or
to Joshua when answers were needed.

And what peace I found in this. At night I inhaled
the sweet scent of my fir bough bed and slept the slum-
ber of the angels.

We were as one in this sisterhood of faith, and here,
for a little while, with Joshua as our holy leader, we had
our own Heaven on earth, a true Garden of Eden.

CHAPTER FIVE

*W*hen my brother Frank and Mollie Sandell decided to get married in July, Mollie approached Joshua just outside the big shelter and asked him to perform the ceremony.

He refused.

"I don't believe in marriage," he said.

Everyone in earshot of this exchange stopped to listen. How could a man of God not believe in the sanctity of marriage?

"It's unnecessary," Joshua went on, acknowledging with a sweeping look our eavesdropping. "A legal convenience devised by men, not by God."

What was he saying? Puzzled, I glanced at the others, who also seemed perplexed.

Joshua smiled, taking a seat on his usual stump. "Think," he said with exaggerated patience. "A man marries you and what does he get? A woman in his bed."

My face flamed. To say that! Right out loud!

"A cook in his kitchen," he continued. "A slave to scrub his floors and wash his clothes. And the force of the law to back him up. A law that says a wife *must* do these things."

We exchanged glances, flustered. All except Aunt Nell, who fixed her burning eyes on Joshua, her lips slightly parted.

"Why do you suppose," Joshua added, "it's known as wed*lock*?"

A few rolled their eyes at each other knowingly, but all I felt was dismay. Truth to tell, I had always looked forward to being a bride. Now Joshua's pronouncements left me feeling childish and guilty.

I was even more confused when Frank and Mollie quietly let it be known they would get married anyway. Was I the only one who had trouble sorting out his rules?

The order about flowers, for instance. Several of us younger girls had skipped into the grove one evening wearing wildflower garlands in our hair—twinings of roses, daisies, buttercups—and I thought we looked lovely. When Joshua commanded me to come to him, I was pleased to be singled out and, unaware of what awaited me, ran to him.

"You will not crown yourselves with flowers!" he burst out, tearing the garland from my hair and throwing it on the ground. "*You* are the flowers of my field."

"I'm sorry, Joshua," I cried, falling humbly to his feet. "I didn't know."

But later I realized I *still* didn't know. What did he even mean? I liked being called a flower of his field, but what had that to do with wearing garlands? I didn't see the harm in it. And why did he have to choose me to shame?

If only my willingness to understand the rules would translate into the ability to do so!

Our immediate family made a trip home for Frank and Mollie's wedding, which would be at our house, with Justice Holgate meeting us there to officiate. Mollie's boardinghouse wouldn't do, of course, and she and Frank weren't about to set foot in any of the local churches.

"There'll be lots of flowers blooming at the house now," I said as we rode toward town in the hired carriage, our first time off the island in five weeks. "I could make a garland to twine down the staircase. And bouquets for all of us."

"No, Eva," Mollie said. "We just want to get this over with as quickly as possible."

I sighed, regarding my soon-to-be-sister-in-law unhappily. Maybe it was selfish of me, but I wanted her to play the part of the happily blushing bride with more conviction. Instead she just sat there, looking put upon, her lank brown hair hanging from her careless bun. The gray gown she wore wasn't even her best dress, much less anything you'd call bridal finery. Heaven help us, if we had to be uncomfortable in these corsets, couldn't we at least be pretty?

"When did flowers become something evil?" I pouted.

"Will you give it up?" Frank said, annoyed. "Flowers aren't the issue. We just don't want any fuss, that's all. We're only making the marriage legal to keep Pop from going completely crazy, all right? I don't want to be there one minute longer than necessary."

"Right," Maud said. "No use letting him get started on why we shouldn't go back to the island."

"And of course," Mama whispered to me, "we won't say anything to him about . . . well, what Joshua said on the subject of marriage."

I nodded resignedly. More and more, not saying much about anything seemed the safest course.

The ceremony was short, without music, and lacking in any charm whatsoever — certainly not the sort of wedding I'd dreamt of for myself. Well, dreamt of before Joshua got me so confused about it, that is.

The only person who seemed truly happy that day was Papa — mainly, I suspect, because he was so glad to see us all. But for me, his touching delight at having us home only served as a guilty reminder of our having left him in the first place. I could hardly wait to get away from his soft looks. I wanted to be back on the island and out of these miserable clothes. The instant our buggy passed through the gate that evening, I had my shoes unbuttoned and off, and my toes were wriggling free.

As it turned out, most of the married women in our group were even more disturbed than I by Joshua's comments on marriage. Shortly after our return to the island, Aunt Hattie actually dared to question him on the subject.

"You have stated," she said in front of the entire gathering, "that to become one with God we must give up all that is unnecessary. And now you've said marriage itself is unnecessary. Are we to infer that we should give up our marriages?"

Joshua smiled. "Only if you want to become one with God."

I glanced around. We *all* wanted to be one with God, didn't we?

Aunt Hattie shot a troubled glance at Aunt Nell, who shook her head warningly.

That evening as I helped the two of them ready their children for bed, I heard them quarreling.

"It doesn't sound right to me," Hattie insisted. "The things he's saying."

"You just don't understand," Nell said.

"Maybe not," Hattie replied, "but if I can't understand it, I'm certain I won't have any luck making Clarence understand it."

"Well, *Clarence.*" The way Nell said his name, with such disdain!

There was a tense pause as I buttoned up little Rachel's nightie.

"He *is* my husband, Nell."

"And Bert's mine. So what?"

I can't say who might have overheard and carried the news of this conversation to Joshua, but learn of

Hattie's doubts he did. The very next morning he gathered all of us as witnesses and then confronted her.

"Pack up, Hattie Starr."

"What? But, Joshua—" Hattie glanced at Nell, who quickly lowered her eyes.

"Do not speak! I've already sent for a wagon. I will not have a woman like you defiling the pure in heart of my church!"

Aunt Hattie's mouth pressed into a thin line. Lifting her chin, she turned and went to round up her boys and her belongings.

When she was ready to depart, we gathered behind Joshua. How frightening he looked, pointing her way out across the slough. Frightening and magnificent, like the angel ordering Eve out the gates of Eden.

"Go back to the sinners and the infidels. We have no use for you here!"

From the loaded wagon, surrounded by her sons, Aunt Hattie looked over her shoulder at us. No one bid her good-bye or offered any word of understanding, not even me, her own niece. We just stood silently, watching the wagon and horses splash through the water and haul up on the far bank.

"Never dare come back to us!" Joshua thundered after her. "From this day forward your soul is cursed to hell!"

Oh, I was so glad it was her and not me on the other side of the slough. To be thrown out of the garden! To be cut off from the sisterhood we'd come to depend upon! Just the thought of it made me desperate for some way of proving my faithfulness to Joshua.

Perhaps Sophie felt the same way, for in the candlelit grove that evening she threw herself to the ground, thrashing until her dress and hair were in tangles. Then she leapt up, proclaiming before us all that she would never let Brother Campbell defile her with a single touch of his hand. She was breaking her engagement with him.

"God told me to," she sobbed. "God spoke to me and I must obey!"

Joshua flung his arms around her and preached up such a sermon extolling her virtue in this sacrifice that I was overcome with envy. If only *I* had an engagement to break off! All I had was a father to defy, and everyone was doing that.

But Joshua delivered an even more startling revelation that night. He too had received a message from God. Preparing us to hear it, he bid us all come sit close and quiet around his feet.

"I've been favored with a message of the gravest import," he said when we were settled, "a message no one on earth has heard for almost two thousand years."

A shiver ran down my spine. I noticed that even the crickets had suddenly gone silent. Every breath was held; not a leaf rustled in the cottonwoods.

"One of you," Joshua said, "one of you sitting here at this very moment will be the mother of the Second Christ."

A sharp intake of breath.

"One of you," he repeated. "Whoever will be found to be the purest and the best, will be the next Mary."

A stir went through the grove, as if the air had been fanned by the wingtips of hovering angels. Every face was lifted to Joshua, rapt and attentive.

"We will discover the Second Mother," he said, "by the most careful testings of faith. Each of you must work to be the best, the purest you can be, the most fitted to wear this sacred crown."

Now our eyes darted about, wondering, *Who?* And *Might it be me?*

"I," Joshua said, "I have been chosen to deliver the Holy Spirit."

A tremulous sigh escaped me. Of course. I should have known. I should have seen it coming. Hadn't I sensed, from the moment we met and he took my hand in his, that he had come into our lives for a reason? That there was some purpose behind all that had been puzzling me? Now it had been revealed, and we sat with smiles of dazed wonderment as we tried to absorb this miraculous news.

One languid afternoon shortly after Joshua's prophetic announcement, I was minding Aunt Nell's babies at the edge of the meadow. With me was Florence Seeley, one of the other younger girls. She was an orphan who'd come down from the mountain hamlet of Alsea with her older sisters, Rose and Edna. I liked Florence, and it was pleasant there where the air was warm and rich with the smell of ripe peaches from across the slough. We had rigged flour-sack hammocks in the trees, and as we idly rocked little Gertie and Rachel, we'd been engaged in only the most inconsequential of conversations. Finally, though, I could hold back no longer from the subject that had been obsessing me.

"Now that Mollie's married," I began tentatively, "do you think she can still be the Chosen One? Or does it have to be one of us unmarried girls?"

Florence thought a moment. "Unmarried, I'd say. The Virgin Mary wasn't married. Not when the angel first came to her anyway."

I nodded. "That's what I've been thinking too."

So who, *who* was it going to be?

Ever since Joshua's revelation, I couldn't stop going over the possible candidates.

Esther was the obvious choice, but then, Joshua hadn't said anything about the Second Mother being the prettiest.

At the same time, I ruled out Rose Seeley, Florence's sister, for being too stout. All three Seeley girls were red haired and ruddy faced, and Rose in particular had the most amazing arm muscles. She worked as a hired girl at the Kline house, as did Attie, and obviously she was no stranger to the chopping of cookstove kindling. But health and heartiness were probably not likely considerations for the Second Mother, and Bible engravings of Mary never showed her anything but slender.

Sophie Hartley? Well, certainly nobody was more effusive in her devotion to Joshua.

Florence herself? Personally, I thought she was a darling; I loved her big blue eyes and strawberry blond ringlets. She had a husky voice that sounded so quaint coming from such a small person. Still, whoever saw a painting of a Madonna with freckles and a little chip in her front tooth that showed when she grinned?

It could be Maud, I suppose. With her dark hair and solemn eyes—yes, I could picture it. And she probably deserved the honor. All those sick children she'd nursed. To be honest, I could think of no good reason it *shouldn't* be Maud except . . .

I wanted it to be me!

If it had been anything else, I would never have dared imagine myself worthy. But, the Second Mother? I *loved* babies. Maybe this was a role in which cleverness wasn't necessary.

Just think! To be the mother of another Christ! I could hardly bear to contemplate the whole glorious prospect, it gave me such a confusion of wonder and fear.

"Do you think it'll be like the first time, Florence? With an angel and all? And the baby just starts somehow, from the Holy Spirit?"

"I suppose."

I picked up my baby cousin Gertie. What bliss, that soft head drowsing on my shoulder, the delicate breath against my neck. Oh, I *had* to be chosen.

Joshua was always reminding us that we were

being tested for Second Mother even when we didn't know it, even when we thought no one was watching. Further, he said the *true* test for each would come when we received word to appear before him alone, in his private shelter.

Ever since I heard that, I'd been praying constantly for the wisdom to face this particular challenge. I just had to do well! And I felt sure I'd have a better chance if only I could master the wisdom of his teachings.

"Florence?" I said now. "Did you understand the sermon this morning? The part about King David lying with Bathsheba?"

"Well, it surely surprised me. Nobody ever told me *that* Bible story before!"

"And Joshua made it sound as if that were a good thing. But isn't that adultery, lying with another man's wife?"

"That sounds right, but I suppose if Joshua says—"

"What's going on here?" It was Esther, coming from behind the trees.

"Oh!" I said, clutching the baby. "Esther! You startled me!"

"What were you two whispering about? It didn't sound like praying."

"But we were," Florence promptly fibbed. "Before."

Esther looked suspicious. "I should probably report you. You're not supposed to be going off on your own. Remember the part in the Book of Timothy about avoiding profane and vain babbling?"

"Oh, please don't report us!" I pleaded, instantly picturing myself at the slough, banished by a wrathful Joshua. "We were . . . discussing scripture. King David and whether what he did was right."

"You're questioning King David?"

I glanced at Florence. "Well, he did get Bathsheba with child."

"So?"

"That's wrong, isn't it?" I said tentatively. "She was another man's wife, and it isn't as if it says anything about Bathsheba being with child because they were expecting the Second Christ or anything."

"How could it, you silly?" Esther said. "The first Christ hadn't been born yet."

"Oh, that's right." How I hated appearing stupid in front of Esther.

"You see, Eva," she said as if I were a five-year-old. "This is exactly why Joshua doesn't want you discussing these things on your own. He wants to make sure he's there to guide you. Besides, with true faith you simply let yourself *feel* Joshua's message in your heart. To pick it all apart word by word is a sin in itself."

"I'm sorry. Truly." Why did Esther always seem so far beyond me in understanding and wisdom? I nuzzled the baby, burying the shame of my flaming cheeks in her softness. Suddenly I thought of a sort of peace offering to Esther. I looked up. "Do you want to hold the baby?"

"Not now. Joshua wants me."

And without even a glance at this darling child, her own niece, she turned on her heel and left. What was she going to tell him? Was I going to be in trouble?

The next day Mollie came announcing I was to appear before Joshua in private. Was I to be reprimanded at Esther's request, or was this my special testing time?

Either way, I was nervous, and my stomach churned as I padded along the path to Joshua's shelter.

"I'm here," I said softly, standing by his tent flap. "It's me, Eva Mae."

"Eva," he said. "Little Eva Mae." I loved the way he said my name. "Come in."

I pulled back the flap and stooped to enter into the darkness. I had not been in his hut before and wondered if it would be different from the others somehow, holy, because it was his. My eyes strained for something to fix on. Only by shafts of light through the gaps in the branches could I make out where he sat.

"Why have you come?" he said.

"Why?" I blinked. "Well, because you called me, Joshua."

He laughed softly. "I don't think that's the reason."

"Isn't it?"

"No. You came because you wanted to. Because something inside you told you to. *God* told you to. Isn't that right?"

I hesitated. What was the proper answer? "Yes,

it's God's will," I murmured.

"And are you willing to show yourself a faithful servant of the Lord by receiving His word through me?"

"Of course, Joshua. You know I am." More than anything I wanted to be good and faithful, pure in spirit, and in so being, earn his love.

"Sit down here," he said, taking my hand. I sank to the canvas-covered fir boughs and waited, nearly paralyzed with anticipation. When would we begin the tests of biblical knowledge, the inquiries of faith? Or was this already an inquiry of faith and I was too ignorant to recognize it?

Now I felt his hand on my shoulder. Good. I hadn't displeased him too much. Maybe Esther hadn't told on me after all. Oh, it meant so much to me to at least be considered for Second Mother. I knew I wasn't the prettiest or the smartest, but I was good with children, and I honestly felt no one could be trying harder to be worthy.

"Lie down," he said.

"What?"

"Here, that's right," he said, guiding me, easing me back.

Was he—? I cried out, startled. He was pulling up my smock! His hand was—

"Now, Eva," he admonished me. "The Lord speaks to me and through me to you. Are you not willing to accept the message?" His voice sounded softer than I'd ever heard it.

"Yes," I whimpered. "But—"

"These are sacred rites, Eva Mae. Secret rites. To even put this into words—ever—would be the purest blasphemy. Do you understand?"

I nodded, scared, and now everything began happening with baffling speed. Murmuring biblical verses I'd never heard, he found the button of my drawers. As he eased them down, my hands instinctively flew to protect those secret places of my person, but he caught my wrists, kissed my palms.

"Eva, be still now," he whispered.

I lay back in shuddering surrender. I didn't struggle as his weight came down on me. Instead it was as if my soul, for a time, took leave of me, took flight.

Afterward I stumbled out into the sunlight, dazed.

How utterly I'd been taken by surprise.

I had expected some holy visitation.

I had hoped for angels.

CHAPTER SIX

For a full three days I drifted as a blind one around the island, not seeing, not hearing. Even when the first shock faded, I remained gravely subdued. I didn't feel like running and laughing along the island paths anymore. Somehow my feet were no longer so light.

Was there something wrong with me? Something depraved that made me unhappy, made me want to question things? Maybe I was just being childish and didn't understand a woman's role, what was required if she were to have a child. Because that much I understood now. All the hints I'd ever heard dropped came together and told me this must be it. This was the act that started babies. Maybe it had to be this way if you wanted to be the Second Mother. Maybe this would be God's way of choosing. The holy mother would be whoever was found to be with child first.

Since to speak of it was forbidden, I didn't confide my experience to any of the others, and likewise, no one came to me. Besides, I knew if I confessed to Maud that the experience had come as a shock, she would reprimand me. "Would Joshua do something that was wrong?" she'd demand, and of course the answer was no. My questioning would bring me no comfort, only more guilt.

So I kept my silence.

August twenty-third was my birthday. I did not expect anyone to mark it; a birthday celebration was surely too self-indulgent. But I cannot deny the little thrill I felt when a delivery boy threw down his bicycle at the edge of the slough, came wading across, and handed me a small gift box from my father.

As the other girls gathered around, curious, I opened it to find the dearest gold heart locket. I let out a delighted little "Oh!" and looked up, expecting similar admiration from my companions. But while Florence, perhaps, seemed a bit wistful, the others drew back with disapproval. Feeling rebuked somehow, I closed the lid. Clearly I wouldn't be wearing the gold heart here.

But in my smock pocket, my fingers stayed curled around the velvet box. Oh, Papa. Just thinking about him made tears spring to my eyes.

Now it was time to leave the island, for soon the autumn rains would swell the channel slough and make access difficult.

How strange it felt, lacing up my corset again, pushing my feet into my toe-pinching shoes. My stomach churned the entire five-mile wagon ride home. I was not the same girl who had climbed into this wagon so gaily back in June. Would my father be able to see that?

Apparently not. When the wagon pulled into our yard, Papa came bounding out of the house.

"Oh, this is good," he said, helping Mama down. "It's been too long, my dear. I'm so glad to have you all back. Eva!" He put his hands round my waist and lifted me over the side. As he set me on my feet, I found I couldn't meet his eyes, and when he hugged me, I went stiff.

"What's the matter, sweetheart?"

"Nothing," I said, but something in my chest felt leaden.

"Say, where's the locket I sent out?" he asked. "Don't tell me that boy never got there!"

"No, I got it Papa. Thank you." I glanced at him. "I'll wear it, now I'm home."

Having missed us terribly, he said, Papa was eager to keep us close and offered our own house for our services and what Joshua was now calling the Bride of Christ Church. A room was cleared for Joshua to sleep in, and most of the girls moved into our house as well, bedding down on pallets wherever space could be found. After being together on the island, the girls going back to their parents' houses wouldn't have felt right. Everyone wanted to keep on devoting themselves full time to our religion. Everyone wanted to stay close to Joshua.

He encouraged us in this and suggested group members remain at our house at all times.

"Whenever you walk out into the sin of the world," he explained, "you risk polluting yourself with their filth and degradation. Because they *will* speak against me. They will try to turn you away from me, but you must be strong against them. You must purify. Purify yourselves for me!"

Also at this time he began to stir something new into his sermons—a terror so pure, a fear so black it made me forget about everything else.

"'And I looked,'" he read from the Bible one day, "'and behold a pale horse: and his name that sat on him was Death, and Hell followed with him. And power was given unto them over the fourth part of the earth, to kill with sword, and with hunger and with death, and with the beasts of the earth.'"

Joshua looked around at us. "You've heard these verses preached before."

I nodded along with the others.

"But I have seen signs! I have seen wonders! God has spoken to me and the time is at hand. These won't just be words anymore. These are marvels you're going to see with your own eyes very soon."

That night in our room, which Maud and I now shared with several girls, I whispered to Attie in the darkness. "Do you really think the world is going to end?" I was hoping she'd say I'd misunderstood.

But it was Esther who took it upon herself to deliver the grim answer. "Of course it's going to end. We *want* it to, remember?"

"We do?"

"What do you think you're asking for, anyway, when you say the Lord's prayer? 'Thy kingdom come, Thy will be done, on earth as it is in Heaven?' You're asking for the Apocalypse."

"Oh." I'd always thought we were simply praying about being kinder to each other. "But the part about everyone else being left behind?"

"What about it?"

"Well . . ." Wasn't it obvious? "My father."

"He'll be left, that's all." Her matter-of-fact voice in the darkness chilled me.

"Esther, don't be so hard on her," Attie said, reaching over to pat me. "Eva, your father may see the light yet."

"Worry about yourself, Eva," Maud joined in. "Not Papa."

"I think it's exciting that we'll be right here to witness the End," Esther said. "I'm looking forward to it."

The End of the World.

I felt sick.

I made it my crusade to win Papa to our side.

"Please join us, Papa," I begged him. "I can't bear to have you apart from us. When Joshua reads those verses about one person being taken up and another left behind, I get so scared."

"My dear. I hate to have you worrying about that."

But I did.

I tried to find comfort in the parts of Joshua's sermons where he reassured us that all who followed him would be saved, but too often he emphasized the uncertainty of everything, saying we could not know at what hour our Lord would come, nor could we know who would be chosen. Before long, my terror was constant. I feared being swept from the earth — I feared *not* being swept.

I expected Mother, Maud, Frank, and Mollie would be saved. But I worried about myself. Surely God would see my doubts even if I hid them from Joshua.

And, of course, I worried about my father. It is one thing, after all, to vaguely fear for a person's immortal soul when you imagine his personal day of death and judgment to be far in the future. Quite another if the reckoning might come for everyone by sundown.

We had to be ready.

So I kept after my father. He'd always put great stock in the Bible, and I used this to my advantage, finding persuasive verses to make my case.

"My dear, dear girl," he would say, smiling fondly when I pointed out a particularly compelling bit of scripture to him. "You're absolutely right. It's all there in the Good Book, isn't it? This talk of giving up worldly goods?"

Hour after hour I prayed, begging God for the sweet peace I knew I'd find when everyone I loved believed the same thing.

And then, a miracle. God must have heard and touched Papa's heart, because finally, in late October, that wonderful day came.

"A man can't serve two masters," Papa declared, and gave notice of quitting his job at Kline's Department Store. He'd been living in sin, he told Mr. Kline, and would henceforth devote himself to our group.

What joy and celebration!

"From now on I'll be doing God's work," Papa announced, and I helped him nail signs on our picket fence and over the door: POSITIVELY NO ADMITTANCE EXCEPT ON GOD'S BUSINESS.

Thus fueled in spirit, our entire group began a fire of purification right there in the yard, launching a frenzy of housecleaning to its most extreme. Previous nights, Aunt Nell and Sophie and Cora Hartley had burned their worldly goods in their own yards, but this fire, with my father's conversion as the centerpiece of the celebration, would be the biggest, most thrilling one yet.

"All to the flames!" Joshua cried. "Every useless piece of clutter that stands between us and our God!"

Onto the roaring bonfire we threw old chairs, boxes of trash, worn carpets, every broken thing we had always meant to fix but never would. With particular glee I tossed in the tattered lace curtains. I'll never have to mend them again, I thought as the flames flickered high.

"If you don't need it," Joshua cried, "destroy it! Let God, not man, provide!"

Just as Frank sent his bicycle crashing into the fiery heap, James Berry drove up in his new auto. At the sight of our spectacle, he jammed on his brakes, pulled off his driving goggles, and stared.

Maud stared right back at him until he shuddered, shook his head, and cranked his steering wheel, turning the auto around.

"You see?" she said to me. "Have you noticed how he is with that contraption? It's like his own personal golden calf to worship. How could Papa ever have thought him a fit husband for me?"

We watched him drive away, scattering pedestrians as he crossed back over the Mary's River bridge.

"I never liked him from the beginning," I said.

Maud gave me a sideways smile. "You didn't, did you?"

I studied her face in wonderment. Was it possible? Yes! I'd said the right thing! Thrilled by this tiniest hint of approval from my sister, I spun and dashed back into the house for more offerings to burn.

How clean the place felt now! The clicks of my heels on the bare wood floors echoed sharply as I whirled through. There was space to move; you could actually breathe. Such purity and simplicity! Why hadn't we done this long ago?

I went upstairs and from the little cupboard in the hall grabbed my prize guitar. Then I skipped down, ran across the yard, and hurled it onto the flames. Never more would it mock me with my inability to play. And besides, who needed this pitiful reminder of my Salvation Army days?

We were still burning things when darkness fell. My blood raced with the chill of the autumn air, the tang of smoke, and the heat of the bonfire. Our faces glowed golden as we circled the blaze.

The idle and curious, earlier just a trickle over the Mary's River bridge, had now grown to a crowd, and above the fire's crackle, we could hear their jeers.

Well, let them laugh, I thought. They'll be sorry in the end.

"Mr. Hurt!" a reporter called. "Will you give us a statement for the paper?"

"Read the sign," my father answered. "I don't consider *The Corvallis Times* to be God's business, do you?"

"Ignore them," Joshua boomed, his glorious hair shining like a halo in the firelight. "Look into your own hearts instead. Pluck out the sin of vanity and rid yourself of every token of it! Give all to God!"

I watched Sophie trip up to him and say something, and I felt a stab of envy as he lay a loving hand on her shoulder. I didn't like remembering what happened in the hut, but whenever I saw him touch someone else, I felt how sorely I still craved his approval.

"What did you tell him?" I begged Sophie as she passed by me.

Her eyes shone. "About the fire Mama and I had. How my brother tried to stop us, but we just went right on."

"Ah," I nodded, wishing I had some dramatic deed of faithfulness to report.

"Now my brother's so upset," Sophie said, "he's telegraphed my father to come home from the mines." She shivered with pleasure. "You should have seen us. Mama and I broke every dish in the house except the plain white china. Her whole wedding set! Wait until Papa finds out. And what we didn't burn or break, we sold. We're giving all the money to Joshua!"

"Aren't you afraid?" I asked, thinking of the stern and foreboding Lewis Hartley. How fortunate that my own father was now with us in our faith.

"Nothing can frighten me," she replied serenely, "as long as I have Joshua. No matter what Papa says or does, to me it's only another chance to prove my faithfulness."

From the crowd in the darkness came shouts. "Why are you doing this?"

"It's God's will!" Maud shouted back, hurling a section of picket fencing onto the fire.

"Bunch of lunatics!"

"Idiot Holy Rollers!"

"Pay them no mind," Joshua said, coming straight toward me.

My heart seized up at his approach, but, as so often happened, he passed me for Esther, his eyes boring into hers. He reached out and seized the scrap of lace collar at her throat, tearing it away. Mesmerized, I watched as, never taking her eyes from his, she began yanking the fancy buttons from her bodice, throwing them into the flames.

"Yes!" Joshua breathed, still intent upon her. "Yes, that's right! Give all to God."

He whirled on with his exhortations to burn, leaving Esther leaning against the cherry tree, breathing hard, heedless of her exposed camisole.

What? I thought wildly. What could I give up? I needed to make some dramatic sacrifice, because I wanted . . . I wanted . . . Oh, I didn't know *what* I wanted.

Well, I *had* burned the guitar. But no, that wouldn't count. Everyone knew I hated that instrument. I had to find something I loved, something hard to give up.

Suddenly I had an idea. Ducking behind the tree, I hiked my skirt and unbuttoned my fancy petticoat, the one Maud always mocked, and let it fall around my ankles. Then I stepped out, snatched it up, ran and tossed it in the fire. The sateen glowed for an instant as it went up in flames. Ah, perfect! Its blackening seemed like the purification of my soul.

Radiant and uplifted, I turned back to Esther and Maud, hoping too that Joshua had seen.

"That was a five-dollar petticoat!" I told Esther.

"Oh, Eva," Maud said, disgusted.

Esther glanced heavenward. "I can't believe she'd even *say* that."

"What do you mean?" I said, stung.

"Don't you even listen when Joshua speaks?" Esther was staring at the fire, and I could see the flickers of flame dancing in the blackness of her pupils. "Remember when he said all that has price contaminates the spirit and hinders communication with God?"

I blinked. "But that's why I threw it away."

"Eva, Eva." She shook her head pityingly. "Don't you see? The fact that you had to *mention* the price shows how far you are from the purity Joshua requires." Now she mimicked me. "'My five-dollar petticoat!' That's boasting. That's the sin of pride."

I stabbed my toe at the trampled grass and glanced around, hoping the shouting and the crackling of the fire would prevent anyone else from overhearing this chastisement Maud and Esther saw fit to lay upon me.

"I didn't mean to boast," I said contritely.

"And what about this?" Maud flicked at my gold locket.

Startled, I grasped the pendant protectively.

"Adornments are sinful," Maud said.

"Maud! It's not an adornment. It's a . . . token of affection. You know that." I turned to Esther. "Papa gave it to me."

Esther smiled coldly. "Perhaps you're forgetting Luke fourteen. 'If any man comes to me and does not hate his father and mother, wife and children, brothers and sisters, yes, and his own life also, he cannot be my disciple.'"

"But my father's with us now. I don't have to choose. Tell her, Maud."

I followed Maud's gaze to the porch, where Papa stood watching. Oh, why couldn't he have been down by the fire at this moment, throwing something into it? I wanted him to look more involved. More a participant and less a spectator.

Esther shook her head. "You don't understand at all, do you?"

Apparently I didn't. Clutching the locket, I stared miserably into the flames. What about *Honor thy father and mother?* Didn't that count anymore?

Esther regarded my hesitation with contempt. "Keep it, then. If you can't give it up with the loving heart God demands, it doesn't mean anything anyway."

"She's right," Maud added.

I bit my lip hard, considering, then tore off the gold heart, ran over, and threw it in the fire. "There!" I cried, but when I looked back, they weren't even paying me any attention.

Now I stared into the embers, waiting for the rush of good feelings due me for this sacrifice. None came. Watching the heart melt, I felt as if I'd thrown my father himself into the fire.

Suddenly I turned and darted after Esther, grasping her shoulder.

"What?" she said, pulling free as if my touch might taint her.

Like an idiot I stood there—speechless, helpless—for I'd given no thought to what I might say. I only knew I still craved some kind of credit. Then I caught the glint in her hair. The mother-of-pearl comb she always wore.

"Your comb, Esther." See how it feels.

"Oh," she said, carelessly plucking it out. "This? That belonged to my mother?" She curled her lip at me in disdain. "My mother who died when I was just seven?" Without another glance at the pretty thing, she tossed it to the flames. Then, paying me no further mind, she began pulling out all her hairpins, loosing her knot, letting her hair tumble in golden waves down over her shoulders. Her face took on that rapt, other-worldly expression I'd come to know so well. She raised her arms, closed her eyes and began singing, everyone momentarily joining in.

"To cast their crowns before Thee
In humble sacrifice,
Till to the home of gladness
With Christ's own Bride they rise . . ."

Across the fire, I saw Joshua watching her. Her, and her alone.

CHAPTER SEVEN

"*W*e may have to hide her," I heard Mollie say to Frank the next day in the now empty parlor. They were readying the place for services, and Maud had sent me in to help. "Nell said they spent a long time talking to Bert and they were asking questions around town. She's afraid they'll be back."

"Who are you talking about?" I asked, completely confused.

"Esther and Nell's brothers." Mollie didn't even look at me. "From Portland. They're trying to get your Uncle Bert to move Nell and the girls up there. Esther too."

Frank adjusted a window drape. "Do you think they heard about Esther being chosen Second Mother?"

My head snapped around. "It's decided, then? She's the one?"

"Really, Eva." Mollie tossed a broom at me. "Everyone's known that for weeks."

"Oh." I started sweeping the floor, sick. My cheeks

blazed with shame at my own foolish hopes. Of course it was Esther. Still, tears pricked my eyes. Hadn't I tried to be worthy too? It didn't seem fair. I'd yearned for so few things in my life.

Esther. I ground my teeth. No wonder she always wanted to sing "The Voice that Breathed O'er Eden." That part about the bride? She was singing about herself! And when I remembered her indifference to her baby nieces . . . Why, this didn't have the first thing to do with her being motherly, did it?

Puffs of dust rose as I swept, making me sniff. My only bit of consolation was that at least Maud hadn't been chosen either. But then this seemed such an uncharitable, unsisterly thought, it only added guilt to my bitterness.

That night the crowds returned, but their mocking laughter was gone, replaced by rumbles of anger. The newspapers had been printing false stories claiming we'd been burning live cats and dogs and, obviously, people believed them.

A rain of pebbles clattered against the windows as we continued our chanting. *"Be with us O Lord in our hour of need. . . . Be with us O Lord in our hour —"*

A rock crashed through the front window, showering glass.

We screamed and cringed, covering our heads. All except Attie, who sprang for the door as if to do battle.

Joshua caught her by the arm. "We won't give back anger for anger," he said, and commanded everyone to the floor.

We put out all the lights and lay down flat while men beat on the doors and broke the windows, yelling as if they longed to break through and tear us limb from limb.

"Christians have always been persecuted," Joshua reminded us in a low voice. "This is exactly what the early Christians in Rome had to endure. Remember, you are God's anointed."

We *are*, I thought. Sprawled on the gritty wooden floorboards, my face resting on my crossed arms, I took comfort in the dearly familiar voices of my companions murmuring in prayer. I had a place here. Maud had been right when she said our bond was stronger than anything those outsiders could understand. And the more rocks the rowdies threw, the tighter our bonds would grow.

"The day will come when those sinners will regret this," Joshua continued. "On Judgment Day, when that final clarion call sounds, the wrath of God will smite them. They'll be watching in awe as we're swept up into the sky. They'll remember this when they're left behind."

I thought of Mabel, who'd mocked me in the store that day. She'd be sorry.

"'Blessed are ye,'" Joshua quoted, his voice rich and soothing, "'when men shall hate you, and when they shall separate you from their company, and shall reproach you, and cast out your name as evil.'"

The next morning we boarded up the broken windows and began again, strengthened by the knowledge we had endured the long night together.

Now Joshua introduced an intriguing new ceremony, directing Esther to lie on a pallet with a white handkerchief covering her face. With his golden head close beside hers on the pillow, their breaths mingling, he whispered her into a trance, urging her to speak the message he would guide to earth from heaven. The rest of us lay on the floor writing down Esther's words on small tablets as Joshua had instructed.

"Prepare . . . for the last days," she chanted in a breathy monotone. "Make ready for . . . the final judgment. You shall know the End is near by the signs I send. And these shall be . . . great plagues and famines . . . and all manner of destruction by fire . . . "

A knock on the front door startled us.

Mama rose, apologizing, murmuring about persuading whoever it was to leave.

But as soon as she opened the door, Sheriff Burnett and his deputy strode in. The sheriff stopped, transfixed, and gaped at Esther's prostrate form.

"*What* is going on here?" he said, shocked.

"Stay back!" Joshua threw out a warning arm, his face still close to Esther's.

Ignoring him, the sheriff stepped forward and

snatched the handkerchief from Esther's face.

We gasped as Esther bolted upright, staring, like a dead one wakened.

"You!" Joshua jumped up, pointed at the sheriff. "You have profaned a holy moment! I will call down the wrath of God upon you!"

"Is that so?" Sheriff Burnett replied. "Well, I'm calling down the wrath of Benton County on *you*." He held up papers. "An arrest warrant."

"What's the charge?" Mollie demanded.

"Insanity."

After two hours behind closed doors at the courthouse that very afternoon, a panel of two doctors, a judge, and a deputy attorney found Joshua sane, but told him to quit town for his own good, as he had aroused far too much ire among the people of Corvallis. Indeed, rumors of a tarring and feathering had persuaded the sheriff to say he could not guarantee Joshua's safety if he lingered.

"Can you imagine?" Joshua exclaimed upon his jubilant return to our house. "They say I've set myself up as a prophet. As if any man would *choose* this! To be persecuted! To be vilified and scorned!" He seated himself on the floor, Maud, Mollie, Esther, and I gathering around him. "Why, I would turn my back on all this and live the easy life of an ordinary, contented man in an instant if I didn't know, deep in my soul, that I'm here because God chose me for this." Now he lifted his head from his hands and looked at each of us in turn.

"Will you stand by me in this? Will you be faithful?"

"Oh, yes, Joshua," I cried along with the others, hurt to think he might question our faithfulness for one instant. And then in a whisper, I asked, "Will you have to go away like they told you?"

"Never!" he said. "I'm not afraid of the people of this town. As I told those judges, the Lord will take care of His own. We are the Lord's apostles and none can touch us."

As Mollie had feared, the Mitchell brothers came down from Portland again, determined to get their sisters Esther and Nell away from Joshua at all costs. Uncle Bert moved Aunt Nell and their daughters up to Portland, while George and Perry packed Esther off to live with them. After just one night she escaped, though, boarding a return train for Corvallis. She was pursued and caught by her other sister, Phoebe, who hauled her back to Portland and committed her to the Boys' and Girls' Aid Society on the claim she'd been mentally deranged by religion.

I have to confess, I found this all quite thrilling. Although I half hated Esther for being the Chosen One, I loved her too. She was so heartbreakingly brave. Why couldn't I be like that? I was too easily frightened into doing what other people wanted. But Esther—oh, she was a wonder.

One day soon after, my father came home from town to find Joshua in discussion with Mama, Mollie, Frank, and Maud. I, as usual, was simply listening, hesitant to offer any comments of my own.

"Excellent, Mr. Hurt," Joshua said when he saw Papa. "I've been wanting to talk with you. We need to get this business of the house expansion settled."

"Expansion?" Papa said, startled.

"I was thinking we could knock out this living-room wall here," Mollie said, "and add ten feet —"

"No, fifteen would be better," Joshua insisted.

"Now wait." Papa looked baffled. "What are you — I never agreed —"

"And no windows in the new wall," Maud said. "That'll cut down on the prying eyes."

"Hold on here. . . ."

"Mr. Hurt," Joshua said, "we plan on at least twenty new converts in the near future, so more space is essential. We'll get rid of that piano."

"Now stop. I never agreed to any sort of remodeling," Papa said. "And no one touches the piano."

At this he looked to me for support, but I refused to meet his eyes. Pleased as I might be to have the piano spared, I didn't dare take his side against Joshua.

"Papa," Maud said, "you *asked* us to hold the meetings here —"

"Because I wanted you at home."

"And you agreed it was getting too crowded —"

"I never agreed to half the things you people are claiming I did. Now look. I thought if I joined you in all this, we might have peace around here instead of this constant arguing. Instead what do I get? *More* arguing."

"But, Victor," Mama protested.

"I said enough!"

Hearing raised voices, others had crept in, filling the room.

Papa lowered his voice. "As a matter of fact, I was coming home to announce that I've just spoken with Mr. Kline. I'll be returning to work tomorrow."

"Pop!" Frank said over the buzz of disapproval that rose.

Papa shut his eyes. "I've had second thoughts about all of this." He seemed to consider his position an instant longer, then looked at us, sad and tired. "I no longer consider myself a member of this group."

"Oh, Victor." Mama's face went ashen.

My father. He looked so old compared to Joshua. Old and weak. And as I stared at him, the most amazing thing happened. It was like the story of Jesus rubbing mud on the blind man's eyes and then he could see. Joshua had brought the light and now I saw.

My father was a lost soul.

It was the strangest sensation, standing there with the others, looking at my father not as my father, but as the pathetic and unreasonable man he'd become. I'd let my love and childish trust in him blind me. How naive I'd been to think that something as fragile and temporal as love for a father could be more important than love for God. One more proof how right Joshua was in directing us to separate from those who weren't true believers.

My father was doomed.

I saw this, and I felt quite calm about it. And relieved. The weight of worry for him had been so great. To simply give up on him was to shrug from my shoulders a heavy burden. And it was this acceptance on my part that would lead me forth along the path of righteousness. Straight is the gate, I thought.

"This is my house," my father said, "and my family. As of now, my involvement with the Bride of Christ Church is at an end."

Foolish, foolish man.

"Out!" he shouted. "Everyone out right now! Everyone except my own family."

Except he didn't really *have* a family anymore, did he?

CHAPTER EIGHT

The fateful night of January 4 was cold and clear. A full moon shone on the river.

Frank and Mollie had moved out and rented a small house of their own in Linn County, just across the Willamette River from Corvallis. There they welcomed Joshua to continue his ministry. To my father's chagrin, Maud and I had begun spending the majority of our time there with the others, often remaining to eat and sleep as Joshua preferred.

Mama frequently joined services too, but that night, she'd gone home briefly. She still felt guilty, I think, neglecting Papa's meals.

Cora Hartley, in contrast, would have left her husband to fend for himself in an instant, but he wasn't about to give her the chance. She and Sophie were kept home under lock and key.

Esther was still up at the Boys' and Girls' Aid Society. Frank had made several trips to Portland to see her, meeting Nell in secret and trying to arrange a way to free our Second Mother, but so far without success.

Our numbers were small then, that night—just our family along with Attie and Rose and Florence Seeley.

The winter cold penetrated the wood floors, making my bare feet ache. As I rolled in prayer, I felt the chill through my thin dress, clear to my bones. The worse it felt, though, the better, for as Joshua always said, we must know the cold.

"Give us strength," we prayed. *"Give Esther the power of resistance over her jailers.... Help her! Help her hold fast in the presence of our enemies.... Our Esther ... Our saint ..."*

A rap on the door. Before we could do more than trade dazed glances, it burst open, spilling a dozen agitated men into our midst, including Lewis Hartley. And my own Uncle Clarence, Mama's brother!

I rose, hiding my face in the curtains of my hair.

"What's your business here?" Frank demanded.

"Him!" Mr. Hartley said, pointing at Joshua. "Put on your shoes and get your hat."

"What'd I tell you?" Uncle Clarence murmured in disgust. "They're barefoot." He shook his head. "What kind of sick business ..."

All of them stared, clearly unnerved by our plain loose dresses and unbound hair.

Joshua stood straight, his eyes at nose level to Mr. Hartley. "I suggest we all pray."

"We've had enough of your kind of praying," Mr.

Hartley replied. "Come on, let's get going."

"Now wait, wait." Was that fear in Joshua's voice? "May I ask where you propose to take me?"

"Just do as you're told," Mr. Hartley answered.

Attie started us on a hymn of dark, minor measures: *"Delay not, delay not, Oh, sinner, take care. . . ."*

As we sang, Mollie moved from one intruder to the other, staring into each face as if to memorize it for future reference. These were not town rowdies, a young ruffian band bent on trouble. These men had been our parents' friends. They were relatives, neighbors, men from behind the counters of various business establishments. They wore no masks, no disguises of any kind, as if they had no call to hide in shame for whatever acts they were about to commit.

Out came the ropes.

Our eyes widened and our voices faltered; Attie urged us to sing on.

The men bound Joshua's hands behind his back, but Uncle Clarence insisted they leave Frank alone.

"That's right," Lewis Hartley said. "This is the one we want." And he shoved Joshua out onto the porch.

"God will smite you for this," Mollie yelled after them.

The instant the door closed, Frank snatched up his shoes and stuck his feet into them. "I'll follow," he said, "and help if I can."

Mollie handed him his coat. "Be careful."

At the window I watched with pounding heart as the moonlit crowd of men hoisted Joshua into a wagon.

Now passed three of the longest hours as we waited and prayed and tried to keep from our minds the visions of what might be happening to Joshua.

Mollie chose our phrase: *"Once again in love draw near, to your servants gathered here."* We chanted this over and over until the words ran together and formed a spell. *"Once again in love draw near . . ."*

We were still on our knees when, sometime around midnight, we heard horses. A moment later the door opened and we scrambled up, struck by the unmistakable stench of tar. Frank brought Joshua in, a blanket around his shoulders, and with soft cries and weeping, we surrounded him.

"Let's see what we can do with this stuff," Frank said, producing a can of turpentine and a bottle of linseed oil.

Joshua lowered his blankets. Oh, what a heartrending sight was our prophet, his poor flesh burned and blistered, his eyes wild with the fright of it all.

"This is barbaric," Maud said, guiding him to a stool. "Tar and feathers. I didn't think anyone *anywhere* did such things anymore." She began picking at what had been, until this evening, the contents of several down pillows.

"Get some rags," Frank told Mollie, then he shook his head. "Tell you the truth, I was afraid they were going to hang him."

"Swore they would," Joshua said, his voice hoarse, "if I ever set foot in Benton County again."

"Idiots!" Mollie said. "Dragging you over into Benton County just to kick you out!"

Maud poured oil on a rag Mollie gave her and tenderly daubed at Joshua's shoulder. He lifted his troubled eyes to her.

I caught my breath. He looked just like a picture I'd seen of Jesus suffering on the cross, eyes to heaven.

"Bless you, Maudie."

Maudie?

"You have the touch of an angel."

My sister's face at that moment took on an expression softer than I'd ever seen before. What magic Joshua had, I thought, to bring out such a beautiful glow of love.

I found a rag, pushed in close to Joshua, and tentatively began on his other shoulder. Did I have the touch too? I tried anyway, and although it probably wasn't right, given Joshua's obvious pain, I secretly enjoyed myself that night. I felt important and useful. We were hours and hours taking care of him, and, indeed, I quite forgot the cold in my zeal for performing this holy service.

In the morning I awoke upstairs on my pallet to the sound of horses nickering. Out the dormer window I saw Frank, Mollie, Maud, and Joshua moving toward a livery carriage waiting on the road. I hurried downstairs.

"Where are you going?" I cried from the porch.

"You'll find out later," Maud said.

"But—"

"No arguing, Eva. Just go in and pray for us."

And they were off. I leaned against the porch post, shivering. They were always leaving me behind. They never wanted to tell me their plans. I was expected to take everything on faith. Go in and pray? I don't feel like it, I thought obstinately.

Strange, how last night's drama and passion had disappeared in the gray light of dawn.

Back in the main room only Attie and Rose remained. Florence was still asleep in the corner.

"Did they tell you where they're going?" I asked.

"Just away for a while," Attie replied. "It isn't safe for Joshua here. But remember he's with us in spirit."

After a moment I sighed. "Is there any food around? I'm starving."

"You think far too much about what you're going to stuff in your mouth next," Rose snapped.

I looked at her. So what was *she* doing—stuffing her mouth *without* thinking about it? Because while I'd been getting thinner, she remained suspiciously stout.

I headed for the door.

"Where do you think you're going?" Rose said.

"Just away for a while," I said, mimicking Attie,

and added coldly, "I'll be with you in spirit."

I boarded the ferry alone and made my way through town to our house, there to tell my waiting mother the story of the terrifying night and the mysterious morning departure.

TAR AND FEATHERS FOR HOLY ROLLER

Creffield Handled Roughly by Citizens of Corvallis.

CREFFIELD AND MISS HURT WED

Corvallis, Ore., Jan.5.—Joshua Creffield, the Holy Roller, who has made the name of Corvallis famous from the Pacific to the Atlantic, last night met the fate which he long had been promised. Tar and feathers in unlimited quantities and without consideration as to expense were administered to the contortionist, and with the "dressing" went an order for the apostle to never again return to the peaceful little city in the valley. Corvallis is rejoicing over the proceedings of last night, and the citizens are congratulating themselves upon having accomplished a good job . . .

WERE MARRIED IN ALBANY

County Judge Palmer Tied the Knot for Creffield and Miss Hurt.

Joshua Creffield and Miss Maud Hurt were married in the court house by Judge H. M. Palmer at 11:30 o'clock yesterday forenoon. They drove to Albany accompanied by Frank Hurt and wife . . .

The Albany Herald

CHAPTER NINE

*M*arried!

Joshua and Maud were *married*!

I couldn't believe it. Marriage wasn't necessary. Joshua said so.

And then he chose Maud!

What would Esther say when she heard? *She* was supposed to be the Second Mother. Did this mean Joshua had changed his mind? For myself, I'd never for a moment dreamt of being Joshua's wife. I never thought he'd marry anyone! But now that he'd chosen Maud . . .

Oh, there it was again, that dreadful feeling — envy, like a serpent, gnawing at my heart. Somehow it felt like Maud had won. And I'd lost.

"It's a shock, I'll admit," I overheard Papa telling Sophie's father when he came out to hear for himself if the newspaper story was true. "But they're of age, Lew. They didn't need my permission."

"Permission? I'd have run him off with a gun if it was *my* daughter."

"Oh, I know. Don't think I'm not puckered. But maybe we should be glad he's taken the conventional route. Maybe it's a blessing in disguise. At least he'll have to give up his ranting against marriage."

"Well, yes, that would be something. I *am* a bit weary of Cora quoting him on the subject."

"And after all, Lew, he is my son-in-law now. I may just have to make the best of it."

That's when it occurred to me: Joshua was my brother-in-law. How strange. Just as I could never imagine whatever family he'd known in the past, I still had trouble thinking of him as a regular person now, forming family ties for the future.

That night I returned to Frank's house.

On the way Ferryman Michael smirked at me. "Hear your little prophet finally got run off for good." He made a mocking pout. "What'll you poor girls do now?"

I stared straight ahead, refusing to give him so much as a glance. What would we do, though? We'd all grown accustomed to taking our directions from Joshua. To be without his guidance was to be completely at loose ends.

Frank and Mollie had returned, and we pondered our situation far into the night, all agreeing that it probably wouldn't be safe for Joshua to return for quite some time. Outsiders were watching every move we made, and not just in Corvallis. Esther's brothers had discovered that Frank was trying to free her from the Boys' and Girls' Aid Society in Portland, so they'd shipped her back to their father's place in Illinois.

"If Joshua's going to be gone for a while," Rose said, "maybe I ought to take Florence up to Oregon City. We can always get work in the woolen mills."

"But think how awful it would be," Mollie said, "if Joshua and Maud came back and everyone had run off. It's bad enough that Esther's completely out of reach now."

A long silence ensued, during which I summoned the courage to pose the question that had been plaguing me.

"What if the final days come," I asked, "and Joshua's not with us?"

Mollie and Frank traded troubled glances.

"I've thought of that," Frank said. "But I just can't believe it could be part of the plan."

And so we clung together, Mama and I dividing our time between home and Frank's house, all of us awaiting further direction.

In February Maud came home.

Alone.

She looked a far cry from a honeymooning bride. I don't know what she might have confided to Mama as she stormed through, but for me she refused to answer the simplest question. She went straight to our bedroom, slammed the door, and locked it.

Dispatches by telegraph soon arrived with the answers—for us and for all of Corvallis.

Joshua was being charged with adultery by Uncle Bert. The reports claimed Joshua and Maud had gone to visit the Starr house in Portland, and they weren't there long before Uncle Bert found Aunt Nell in bed with Joshua. Joshua had run off and hadn't been seen since.

"Now will you people see that man for what he is?" Papa raged, pacing the kitchen like a caged beast. "Adultery! Barely married to Maud a full month! Why, I never should have given him the benefit of the doubt for one minute. Adultery!"

"Victor, please," Mama said.

"Poor little Eva Mae here." Papa glanced at me, then turned away, shaking his head, pinching the bridge of his nose. "She probably hasn't any idea what that even means."

I blushed, keenly aware how shocked he'd be at what I *did* understand.

"Deplorable!" Papa cried. "That we even have to discuss such things in our house. That they're getting printed in the paper. Things about our family!" He marched up to the landing outside Maud's room and shouted through the door. "Do you hear me, Maud? It's just lucky for that so-called husband of yours I'm not a violent man! Plenty of fathers would have shot him dead already!"

"Go away!" she yelled from the other side of the bedroom door.

He stomped back down the stairs where Mama and I stood.

"Well," he said, struggling for breath and control of himself. "Can I presume the two of you have had enough now?"

We merely looked at him.

"Answer me. Are you ready to come to your senses?"

"Maybe it's not true!" Mama blurted.

"Not true! Sarah, Bert *found* them."

"We don't know that for sure," I said, defending Mama . . . and Joshua. "You know how the newspapers lie. Or Uncle Bert might be lying."

"Now why on earth would he do that?"

"Well, obviously, to make Joshua look evil!"

Papa gave me a pitying look. "Oh, Eva, my dear little Eva Mae. Trust me. No man would lie about a thing like this. You think he's going to be proud to announce it to the world? That his wife cheated on him?"

But these things were different with Joshua, I was thinking. Outsiders couldn't understand. If I had learned one thing from Maud and the others, it was this: Joshua would not do bad things. Once you understood that, everything was so much easier. But if you started doubting . . . no, that was a path you just didn't dare go down.

"I refuse to believe those newspaper reporters,"

Mama said. "What if people believed all the lies that were written about us?"

"Yes!" I cried. "Remember when they claimed we were sacrificing cats and dogs? And anyway, this is exactly what Joshua said would happen. He warned us people would spread falsehoods about him. He prophesied it."

"Give me strength!" Papa cried. "If he isn't guilty, why's he run off? Why didn't he stay and answer the charges?"

Mama looked bewildered. "I thought Maud said he went back to Albany."

"Well, maybe Maud knows more than the rest of us. But as far as the law goes, he's in hiding, with a reward out for his arrest."

Mama glanced up the stairs. "Oh, poor Maud."

"Poor Maud, indeed," Papa said. "Our poor family." He gripped Mama's shoulders. "Because I did have a family here, Sarah. I had family a man could be proud of. Before that man came along."

Mama twisted away from him, her face hard set. "Maud loves him. Did you ever think of that? Your daughter's in there with a broken heart, and all you care about is how this looks."

"What! I can't believe I'm hearing this! Don't you realize I'm already the laughingstock of this town?"

I crossed my arms, my face set as hard as Mama's.

"If I was one to worry how things look," he said, "I'd have done like Lew Hartley and locked you all up and thrown away the key a long time ago!"

We stared at him, and in the icy blast of our disdain, his belligerence suddenly broke down.

"Oh, Eva, you were my sweet little girl. And now look at you. Why? *Why?* What have I done to deserve this?"

He tried to seize my hands, but I pulled away and clapped them over my ears. I wouldn't listen as he raved on and on. I simply couldn't bear to hear ill spoken of Joshua.

For if Joshua were a bad man, what would that make me?

CHAPTER TEN

*T*hose horrid newspaper men!" Maud cried, flying into our bedroom a week later, still wearing her coat. "I can't go anywhere without them following me."

From downstairs, Papa called up. "Maud, there's a gentleman from the *Gazette* on the porch to speak with you."

"I *know*, Papa! For heaven's sake, tell him to go away!" She slammed the door. "What is the *matter* with him? Will he never learn that no good comes from talking to reporters?"

"Where have you been, Maud?" I said. "What's happening?"

"Oh, Eva." Her cheeks were flushed; she was breathing hard. "Joshua's back."

"He is?" I whispered, awestruck.

She nodded. "And we have to hide him." Then she proceeded to lay bare the most audacious of plans. We would hide Joshua under our very own house! Built to withstand the flooding here at the confluence of the Mary's River and the Willamette, the brick foundation was higher than most, and while it wouldn't afford standing room, it could comfortably shelter Joshua until things calmed down.

"What about food?" I said.

"We'll slip it to him through the crawl space."

"But Maud, what if Papa finds out?"

"He can't, that's all. We absolutely mustn't let anyone find Joshua."

"Would they put him in jail?"

"Or worse."

What was worse than jail? Then it struck me. "Maud! You think they'd actually . . . kill him?"

"Eva Mae." She looked at me as if she couldn't believe my stupidity. "Honestly, how could you have lived so long and learned so little?"

I bit my lip. It just shocked me, that's all.

"Now, Frank's bringing him tonight," she continued. "I'll see to everything—and explain to Mama."

Sometime past midnight Maud rose and crept out. After that I heard nothing, even though it seemed I lay staring into the darkness for hours. I must have slept at last, for when I woke, she was in her bed again, watching me as I opened my eyes to daylight.

I didn't have to ask if Joshua was under the house. I could feel the power of him coming right up through it to our second-story room.

Now began the strangest of times.

From his hiding place, Joshua issued directives

that we might continue to grow in holiness and purity in preparation for the End.

We should return to wearing our island gowns, he said. We should give up wearing any hats and even the use of hairpins. He wanted the locks of his women to hang down as God intended. Nothing should come between our heads and heaven.

And so we drifted along Main Street in our faded smocks, tresses streaming, the long ends brushing our hips. What a wonder—all that hair let loose, masses of unruly chestnut, a silken fall of honey, thick waves of richest dark brown.

Never before had we appeared this way in public. Never before had people seen anything like it.

They stared.

I didn't care. I walked in proud tranquillity, of another world than the one that included Mabel Allen gaping at me as I passed.

"No shoes!" Joshua had also ordered. Nothing should come between our feet and God's earth. So we were barefoot, Maud, Attie, and I, walking right down the boardwalk, stepping off into the cold spring mud that squished between our toes. I felt such a purity of purpose, heading for the ferry landing to go to Frank's, never once glancing in the shop windows at the bolts of dress goods or latest hats.

Gliding along, I felt the eyes of the town upon us as heads turned in our wake.

As we passed Kline's, Papa rushed out.

"What in heaven's name do you girls think you're doing?"

Speak not with the unrighteous, Joshua had warned, so we didn't answer, pausing only briefly to turn and gaze at a place just beyond my father's shoulder.

"For the love of God, will you go home?" he begged, frantic at all the curious faces poking out of stores up and down the street.

We smiled serenely.

"We *are* going home," Attie said as we swept past him.

Later, after we'd returned from our gathering at Frank's, Papa argued himself weary.

"Don't you know you're ruining your chances of making good marriages!"

"I'm already married," Maud said pointedly.

He clenched his teeth. "You'll have to forgive my forgetting, Maud. It's not really much of a marriage, is it? And what about your little sister here? Who'll have her for a wife after this?"

"Maybe I don't want to marry," I said. A year ago that would have been a lie, but now, with the world so close to ending, I had more to think about than courting. I had my own soul to save.

"Well," Papa said, "you'll never be taken on as a teacher or a nurse either with the reputation you're getting. Good Lord! Half the town saw you today, I'll wager, and the other half's heard about it."

I regarded him as if from a distance. "It doesn't matter, Papa."

"Doesn't matter?" His voice rose. "Doesn't *matter*?"

"Those are old rules, Papa. Foolish rules about hats and shoes. In our New World, they won't count."

Joshua mocked the daily schedule of chores until we stopped doing housework altogether. We shoved aside the few remaining pieces of furniture and passed the days sprawled on the bare floors praying, always striving for that mental state most conducive to communication with God.

"What!" my father said. "Am I to put on a pinafore and keep this house myself?"

We didn't answer. We drifted around him as if he didn't exist.

One day Maud returned from slipping Joshua his food and reported he'd given us a new commandment. "We're to give up cooked food," she said. "We must eat only what comes pure, as God intends, from the earth."

When my father presented himself for the evening meal that night, he found us nibbling raw vegetables. "No supper?" he asked plaintively. "None of you will cook anymore?"

We refused to look at him.

"Well, then, if anyone cares, I will be in town, dining at the Hotel Corvallis!"

We didn't protest or beg him to stay. Instead, we started to pray.

Infuriated, he smashed on his hat and stalked out.

Go, I thought. You're nothing to me.

CHAPTER ELEVEN

Florence Seeley was the first to be taken.

A few of us were gathered at Frank's house when her older sister appeared at the door. Edna Seeley had fallen away from our group and left town after the island camp. Now she was back, and she had the sheriff with her.

"What?" Florence's eyes went wide as Edna pounced on her. "What are you doing?"

"What I should have done a long time ago," Edna said, hustling her toward the door as their third sister Rose struggled up from the floor.

"Now just a minute," Frank said, blocking their exit.

"Edna, you can turn to the devil if you want," Rose said. "You don't have to drag her with you."

"She's my sister just as much as yours, Rose."

"Well, this is my house," Frank said. "You've got no business —"

"I've got a warrant," Edna said.

The sheriff confirmed this with a nod. "Insanity."

Edna held up Florence's wrist. "Look at this! My

God, she's nothing but bones. Are you people starving her?"

"No, you don't understand," I said. "This is part of the plan. We're becoming purer. We don't need to eat the way sinners do."

Edna rolled her eyes at the sheriff. "You see what I mean?" Then she turned back to me. "And you look just as puny." She sniffed at Frank. "Too bad nobody in your family is sane enough to get you out of this."

And then Florence was gone, dragged to a waiting carriage as we watched from the window.

"What are they going to do with her?" I asked.

Rose turned away from the window. "Edna's been threatening to haul Florence up to that home for the bad girls where they had Esther."

"But can they do that?" I said, with the first flutterings of fear. It had been a shock when Esther was carted off, true, but she had always seemed like a special case. I hadn't seen her incarceration as the start of a possible pattern for the rest of us. Until now, that is. "Can they just lock people up?"

"Sure," Attie said. "You'd be the easiest of all. At your age, your father can just sign you over. No hearing, no nothing. But then, Boys' and Girls' wouldn't be so bad. I doubt you'd be bedding down with true lunatics anyway. Just the kiddies knocked about by their own mamas and papas, the odd girl in the family way. Better than where I'll be going."

"Attie, where?"

Her lip curled. "Ever hear of the state insane asylum?"

"Oh, no!"

"That's what they're saying," Frank put in.

"But don't you see?" Attie said. "I figure it *has* to be this way. God's working His purpose out. We'll be like the martyrs of old." Her eyes shone. "We can be like Saint Perpetua. She was young when they killed her."

"They *killed* her?" I said.

"What do you think being a martyr is all about, Eva?"

My heart started to pound. Is this how it was going to end for us? I thought we were all supposed to be together with Joshua for a glorious ascension into the clouds. I didn't feel brave enough for some lonely death, all by myself.

"They say Perpetua's father begged and begged her to give up her faith," Attie continued. "All she had to do was make the token pagan sacrifice to the Roman gods and they'd let her go, but she wouldn't do it. No matter how her father pleaded, she just said, 'I'm a Christian and I refuse to deny it.'"

Attie shuddered with a hint of pleasure. "So they tossed her to the beasts and the beasts tore her apart."

Next, James Berry filed a complaint of insanity against Frank and Mollie. We were at our house when we heard the news they'd been thrown into the Linn County jail. My father immediately prepared to go over and sort the whole thing out.

"It's not too late," he said, coming down the stairs carrying a pair of his own shoes and an extra hat. "I still don't believe Frank's truly insane. He's just . . . confused."

No one answered, but Papa talked anyway, as if insisting on his presence even as we tried to deny it.

"If Frank will just put these on and give a few straight answers, I believe we could still avoid this."

This, I now understood, thanks to Attie, being commitment to the asylum.

But Frank, faithful martyr, sealed his own fate by stuffing the shoes and hat in the jailhouse stove and burning them to ashes. He and Mollie were given a quick hearing, promptly declared insane, and taken on the train to Salem.

The state asylum! That's where they put people when the local pesthouse got too crowded—anyone and everyone people wanted to be shut of, diseased people, violent people . . .

For so long I had imagined the men in town powerless against our persistent faith. It had never occurred to me they might simply lock us up. But maybe Attie was right. Maybe this *was* all just part of the plan.

When I whispered the news of the commitments to Joshua during the delivery of his meal, he certainly did not seem at all surprised or alarmed.

"God is working His purpose out," he assured me,

his voice raspy from lack of use. "Each of you who suffers for me will have extra stars in her crown."

My uncle, Ira Bray, took the train from the coast and charged around town brandishing a gun. He was after Attie and went to the Kline house where she still occasionally worked. While he stood on the front porch demanding Mrs. Kline produce his crazy daughter, Attie ran out the back. She rook refuge at our house, and the two of us were there alone just an hour later when we spotted him marching purposefully in our direction over the Mary's River bridge.

"The attic!" I cried, pushing her toward the stairs.

Heart pounding, I opened the door to my uncle Ira a moment later and calmly insisted I had no idea of Attie's whereabouts.

"I'll just bet you don't," he said, pushing past me, striding through the parlor and kitchen.

I knelt in prayer as I heard him upstairs going through the bedrooms. *Don't let him look in the attic*, I prayed. *Don't let him look under the house and find Joshua.*

Finally he came back down.

"Hell of a thing, man having to beg people to lock up his daughter."

I felt him pause beside me. I didn't open my eyes.

"You tell her I'll get her," he said, and stomped out.

Some time later, when it was safe, Attie crept downstairs.

"I'm sure he loves having this excuse to come after

me," she said. "He's never forgiven me for not coming back to the ranch when I finished school, you know. I'm like one more stray milk cow he's determined to round up."

"He wants you in the asylum, Attie."

"Of course! That'll show me, won't it?"

"But you're not insane," I protested.

"That's the beauty of it," Attie said, smiling. "If you're not crazy when they lock you up, you will be soon!"

It was appalling, the way the men of Corvallis ganged up against us. All they had to do was tell the doctors and lawyers and judges we wouldn't wear hats or sit in chairs or cook their suppers, and faster than you could say "Lord in heaven deliver us," papers were signed certifying our insanity.

Even my own father! Misguided as he was, I'd certainly never had any real fear of him, knowing he was essentially a gentle man who wouldn't dream of laying a hand on me. But now he was right in there with the rest of them, making sure we all got properly locked away.

Rose Seeley had put it about that she was leaving town, then secretly joined Attie at our place, the two of them hoping to make the attic a long-term hideout. Papa discovered them in no time at all, however, and marched them straight down to the courthouse. Within twenty-four hours they were on their way to the asylum.

He also joined Uncle Clarence in testifying against Florence, she having no father of her own to do the honors. Lewis Hartley declared his determination to keep his wife, Cora, locked up at home, but swore a complaint of insanity against his daughter, Sophie, and also against Maud.

Finally Papa too agreed that Maud must be committed to the asylum in Salem.

I'll never forget the anguished look she gave Mama and me when they came to put her on the train. She wasn't afraid of the asylum; her only concern was Joshua and what would become of him without her.

"Take care of him!" she whispered to us in the final moment. "Protect him."

I nodded, fervently determined to do my part. But how long would it be, I wondered, before our father signed *me* away?

When he returned from Salem, I confronted him.

"How could you?" I said bitterly, breaking my vow of silence toward the unrighteous. "Your own children. You better pray to God you see the light before the Final Days."

"Oh, Eva Mae." He sank with great weariness to the bottom steps of the staircase, just about the only place left to sit in the house other than the floor. "It breaks my heart to think you're still clinging to this end of the world business. You're an intelligent girl. Don't you realize this is something religious hucksters are forever preaching?"

"Don't *you* realize you're cursing your own soul to hell to call our prophet vile names?"

He sighed. "All right, say he's sincere." He took a

deep breath, proceeding carefully, not wanting, perhaps, to miss this rare chance for actual discussion with me. "Say he really believes what he preaches. In fact, you may not believe this, but I accept that you are all truly sincere in your beliefs."

I gave him my haughtiest glare. He couldn't possibly imagine we were hoping for *his* approval.

"But did you know there was a preacher back in the 1830s who had thousands of people believing the world was about to end?"

I froze, statue still, listening in spite of myself.

"I'm sure he believed it too." My father rose and moved slowly toward me as if approaching a wild animal. "But that didn't make the world end, did it? And there was another preacher who—"

"No!" I careened away from him. "No, I won't listen! That's the devil in you speaking." I struck a stance and thrust my arms to the heavens. *"Now is come salvation, and strength, and the Kingdom of our God, and the power of his Christ!"* I pointed at my father, sighting along my arm as I'd seen Joshua do. *"For the accuser of our brethren is cast down . . ."*

"Eva, Eva . . ."

"And they overcame him by the blood of the Lamb, and by the word of their testimony." My eyes shot daggers into his. *"And they loved not their lives . . ."*

"Eva, stop it!"

"And they loved not their lives unto the death!"

CHAPTER TWELVE

Wake at dawn, open my eyes, stare at the ceiling. Flat on my back on the wood floor, I feel his power rising up through the house, lifting, holding, floating me. Stand and look out the window. Once more the sun. Another day, perhaps the last. Over in that town, that place of sin, the courthouse clock tower juts heavenward. Words carved in stone—omen of doom for those who would heed it: "The Flight of Time." Time is passing. It's almost gone. I want it to be gone, because we're waiting. We've been waiting so long....

Drift downstairs. Eat nothing. Joshua wills it. Only water. Pure water. The body must be as pure as the mind.

Mama looks up from her prayers and says the Power is still with us. Joshua lives.

The others are gone, locked away. We two alone remain.

I take up the Bible and sink to the floor with it. Revelations. The black markings on the pages swirl before me, collecting themselves into images. The great wonder in heaven, the woman clothed with the sun and moon under her feet and upon her head a crown of twelve stars ... the horses with heads of lions, breathing fire and smoke and brimstone . . . the mighty angel clothed in a cloud and a rainbow, right foot upon the sea, left foot on the earth, and the voice of a roaring lion, opening the book . . .

And the book says . . . what? What does it say? What am I to do? How do we save ourselves?

Seized with the fear, the breathing hard and swooning fear.

Oh, blessing and glory and wisdom and thanksgiving and honor and power and might be unto our God forever and ever. Blessing and glory and wisdom and honor and power . . .

Later, hours later, days later? I hear my mother say it's time. That man who thinks he's my father is still gone, over in that town across the bridge and it's time. My turn.

From the floor, I rise. I'm a priestess, a saint, a being of purity and holiness, radiant with light. It's true, all he promised. My footsteps are lighter, my feet barely touch the floor. Daily I'm becoming more of spirit than flesh. From the pantry shelf I take our offering, another glass jar of last summer's fruit. Out onto the porch.

To the east, at the two rivers' confluence, the flouring mills. I gasp, shut my eyes, open them again. Messages in the mist at every turn, now that I truly see. The mill! Two women shall be grinding at the mill: the one shall be taken, and the other left!

I scan the slopes to the Mary's. No one about. On the bridge, a wagon. I wait until it passes down the county road. Holding the jar in the folds of my smock, I edge to the corner of the house, stoop to the pretense of planting new flowers. Another glance over my shoulder and I place my offering on the crawl space altar. After a moment, his pure white hand. Oh, blessed am I among women, to see his holy hand! Esther is not here for this. Nor Maud. I, alone, am the handmaiden of our Lord.

I stand, bracing myself on the porch post against the whirling. And hunger.

No, not hunger. We mustn't be hungry. A craving of the ungodly. "Man does not live by bread alone, but by every word that proceedeth from the mouth of God. . . ."

Inside, I take down another jar of peaches and slop some into a bowl. I stir in flour. That's all our Joshua will eat. Why should I have better?

My mother joins me in this, our sacrament.

And now the evening tests of faith. That man comes home and begins his useless nightly pleadings. Will we come to our senses, for the love of God?

Foolish, foolish . . . everything we do is for the love of God.

He doesn't want to have us committed, but we are wasting away, we are hollow-eyed ghosts, we are dying. . . .

I drift past him, escaping to the porch, there to sit near our Joshua's place of power.

Time passes; the sun sinks, bathing pasture and trees in golden light. On the bridge, a figure. I squint into the evening glow. So far away, and yet how well I know that gait, that swing of the arm. Unsteadily, I stand. Attie. I squeeze my eyes tight, trying to remember. Plain thinking's so hard. But I thought . . . isn't Attie locked in that bad place up in Salem? It can't be her.

But, it is.

Attie.

Or her ghost.

I drift up the lane, meeting her. I'm crying and I don't remember why.

She's embracing me but then putting me aside, aiming herself toward our house, murmuring Joshua, oh, Joshua. If only to be closer to him for one brief moment . . .

That man at our house is the crazy one, turning it all around and around, talking, always talking, pleading and all the time raving, raving. He can't stand it. He can't save us. Attie must go back to the asylum. He's going to have to take me to that other place in Portland. That Boys' and Girls' place . . . He's tying on an apron. He thinks he's going to feed Attie cooked food. He doesn't understand at all. These are the ways of the wicked. . . .

ATTIE BRAY'S JOURNEY.

*Escaped the Asylum and Traveled Afoot to Corvallis—
Her Condition.*

A tedious journey of thirty odd miles on foot, with
nothing but a few strawberries to eat, was an act
Tuesday by Attie Bray, one of the Holy Roller Girls,
recently sent from Corvallis to the insane asylum.
The trip was from the asylum farm to Corvallis and
the distance was covered between four in the morning and seven in the evening. Considering that Miss
Bray is a frail young woman, suffering with a religious mania, the feat takes on the character of the
unusual. She managed to escape from the atten-
dants at the asylum farm about four o'clock in the
morning, and at once started for Corvallis. How
many of the roads she traveled she was unac-
quainted with is not known, but she managed to
thread them with sufficient certainty to reach the
Albany bridge at two o'clock in the afternoon.
Passing over it, she found a secluded spot on this
side, and there rested until four o'clock, after which
she resumed her journey. A few minutes after seven
o'clock, she passed through Corvallis and made her
way to the home of Victor Hurt, south of Mary's
River. There she was given food and kindly treated,
and her arrival reported to the authorities.

Miss Bray is apparently not improved in
mental condition. . . .

The Corvallis Times, June 11, 1904

The devil—that's who he is. He calls himself my father, but only the devil would have dragged me onto the train, brought me to this place, signed papers turning me over to strangers, more devils I don't even know.

Lock me up then. Lock me up if you must, but you will never lock up my spirit. I will pray and I will not listen to you and I will keep the faith.

I must lie on the floor. I must not stop praying. Joshua will know if I stop and God will smite me.

Those girls are staring at me. The woman pulls me up. Come, dear, she says. You must eat.

No, I won't get up. I can't. I can't eat.

Of course you can. You must eat.

No, not your food.

It's perfectly good food.

No! I must know the hunger.

And now some other voice: How long has she kept this up?

Two days now.

Mercy.

Good at it too this business of hanging limp. My back's fair broken trying to drag her around.

Not your food! I cry. Joshua forbids it!

Oh, Joshua again, is it? I'll hear no talk of him, thank you very much. I'm sure we've all had quite our fill about this Joshua from Miss Esther Mitchell.

Esther?

Esther? I sat up, blinking, saw that I was in a large room furnished with plain iron beds. "Is Esther here?"

The two women traded a glance. "Coming round, then," I heard the younger one murmur.

I took several deep breaths. Disinfectant, that's what I smelled. What *was* this place anyway?

"Now, Eva Mae," the older one said, "I'm the matron here at Boys' and Girls' Aid Society. You must call me Mrs. Graham."

I looked at the two women in their starchy pinafores.

"Where's Esther?" I whispered again.

"Oh, she's long gone, dearie. Took her back to Illinois, they did."

That's right. I knew that. Except . . . at the moment I was hardly sure what I knew about anything. I was so sickly weak and disoriented, all my senses were blurred.

"You must be famished, dear," Mrs. Graham said. "Let's just go on down to the dining hall and see if you might not take a bite."

Shakily, I stood. Actually, I was hungry. Terribly hungry. And I didn't have the strength to fight these people anymore. They were so persistent. I let myself be led out into a hall, leaning on their arms so I wouldn't fall.

So Esther was gone, then. But wasn't there someone else? Florence! Hadn't I caught a glimpse of Florence here? Just a flash of her strawberry blond curls?

I was led to a small dining hall filled with children from toddlers up to grown girls like myself, three dozen of them, all seated at tables. I stood in the doorway and inhaled.

Food.

Spotting Florence over by the windows, I tugged feebly to go to her, but Mrs. Graham's grip held tight.

"Let's just sit you down at this table here," she said.

Maybe I'll only pretend to eat, I thought as she pushed my chair in. But I was weak. As she lifted the spoon, my mouth betrayed me, opening on its own as if I were some baby bird.

What a pleasant shock, that first bite. It was only breakfast porridge, but oh, it was thick and rich and they had cream and brown sugar to put on it. The comforting warmth of it sliding down to my stomach was too good to resist. Ignoring the inquisitive looks of the other children and the smiling satisfaction of the matron, I took the spoon from her and began shoveling in one mouthful after another.

❦

After that, I attended meals regularly.

I'll eat, but I won't talk, I promised myself. I'll do what they tell me, but I'll keep my faith. I'll resist them in my heart. And when I'm strong, I'll escape.

It was difficult, though, for with regular nourishment—which I'd not had for two months now—my mind began to clear. I started taking stock of my situation and this place where I'd been deposited. Boys' and Girls' was full of little children, and I felt self-conscious, praying by myself in front of them. When I tried to worship as we used to, rolling on the floor, they all seemed so alarmed, I would give it up, just to calm them. And since the day was divided into closely supervised group lessons or chores, I rarely had a private moment. Even when I did, without Joshua and the others, I found it hard to summon the necessary spirit.

As for Florence, the matron kept steering me away from her, and Florence herself seemed to be pretending not to know me. One day as she pulled weeds in the vegetable garden, I went right up to her, knelt down, and asked her why.

"I'm sorry," she said, dropping a weed clump in her basket. "But they warned me not to talk to you. At first anyway."

She sounded different somehow. She looked different. Her hair, that's what it was. She'd let them bind her curls into a tight thick braid. Mine still hung loose. That was one thing I hadn't given up on.

Florence glanced around, keeping her voice low. "I think they won't mind now, though, because . . ." Her voice dropped until it was barely audible. "Because now I'm cured."

She pronounced this with a certain shame, and when she glanced back over her shoulder, I wasn't sure if it was the girls in the next cabbage row who concerned her or if, like me, she was still forever imagining Joshua watching her, listening to her every word.

"I'm getting out," she continued. "Next week they're letting me go up to my aunt's place in British Columbia."

"But I don't understand. What do you mean, you're cured?"

"Of Joshua."

I couldn't believe I was hearing this. "But Florence, we all —"

"I don't even want to talk about him," she said nervously. "Please."

"But —"

"Just stop it!" She gave me a look of utter torment. "I want to get out of this place, all right?"

As I stared at her, I felt the matron's hand on my shoulder.

"We're going to put you over here in the berry patch," Mrs. Graham said, handing me a basket.

I allowed myself to be pulled up and led away. Kneeling at the spot I was directed, I began plucking the ripe red strawberries, more confused than ever.

❦

Now that I was behaving myself, as they put it, I not only worked in the garden, I was also occasionally sent with the other older girls to the basement laundry room, there to help iron the stacks of linens used in the home. I often saw Florence chattering quite freely with the others, even once in a while flashing a grin. Never at me, though. I was a reminder of Joshua and her betrayal of him, I suppose. I only made her feel guilty.

After Florence left for British Columbia, Mrs. Graham, the matron, began to call me in for little talks every day. It was important for her to know—had Mr. Creffield had illicit relations with me?

I pretended not to understand what she meant, and in truth, I *was* unsure enough that this didn't seem a complete falsehood.

Though I managed to evade her questions, she persisted in talking about Joshua at every opportunity, saying she was always reading about him in the papers. There was a big reward out for his capture—money put up by the families whose wives and daughters he'd led astray. Everyone knew what a bad sort he was.

"Not everyone," I said loyally. I couldn't imagine Maud giving him up. Or Esther.

"Well, my girl, there are very few of you still supporting him, and the numbers are smaller every day. We're so glad that Florence came round, of course, and now we've had word her sister Rose has renounced Mr. Creffield too."

I blinked in disbelief. "She has? Rose?"

Mrs. Graham nodded. "She'll be out of the state asylum any day now."

What was I to make of this?

"But Esther Mitchell," I said. "I'll bet she hasn't given him up." I'd heard from one of the girls here that Esther had kept everyone awake all night with her chanting and praying and had hardly ever let the smallest morsel of food pass her lips.

"Esther. Well, she's a case by herself, isn't she? Set this place on its ear, she did, forever claiming messages from God Himself." Mrs. Graham shook her head. "No, I fear for that child." Then she gave me a tired sort of smile. "But you're a good girl, Eva Mae. You have a family, a father who loves you. We all feel you're going to recover yourself very soon."

She meant this to be comforting, I know, but it wasn't.

"Surely you don't think religion," I ventured, "is something a person should try to recover from."

"Not true religion, dear. But this is a false one. Mr. Creffield only wants you to worship *him*. Don't you see that?"

I didn't know what I saw anymore. Should I believe Mrs. Graham? Except for the bad things she said about Joshua, she seemed a kind and loving lady. But was this just the devil speaking, trying to lure me away? I remembered how hard we'd prayed that Esther would have the strength to resist the people in this place. Think how disappointed in me she'd be to hear I'd given in when she hadn't. Think if Joshua saw me sitting here, wavering. Still, if one by one all the others were giving him up . . .

"Mrs. Graham? If what you say is true, then what is your cure?"

"Oh, we have no cure, my dear."

"No cure? But we can't leave until we're cured, isn't that right? So how can you tell me you have none?"

"We don't need a cure," Mrs. Graham said. "All that's needed is for you to be away from Mr. Creffield. Time, that's all, and you'll come round. We'll just give it time."

One day the Boys' and Girls' Aid Society supervisor, Mr. Gardner, called me into his office.

"Eva Mae," he said, closing the door. "This has gone on long enough. We need for you to tell us the truth now."

Heat rushed through my body; my stomach turned over. The truth? I wasn't sure what that was anymore.

"I realize this has to be terribly painful for you," Mr. Gardner went on. "And you must trust me that I don't want to make things any more difficult for you than they already are. But in order for us to help the children who come to us, we have to understand their situations. You see this?"

Reluctantly, I nodded.

"Very good. Well." He hesitated, apparently perplexed as to how he might continue. "In your particular case—yours and Florence Seeley's and Esther Mitchell's, that is—the authorities are going to want to know . . . that is, if and when Mr. Creffield is found and brought to justice, certain inquiries will be made. Am I making myself clear?"

Not really, I thought, nodding again.

"Now. Mrs. Graham claims you won't answer her questions."

My hands twisted in my lap. Somehow I'd been able to evade her grandmotherly inquiries. But Mr. Gardner was a man of great authority. That was different. It seemed I would have to answer.

"She says you pretend not to know what is meant by criminal relations."

"Well, I don't," I whispered. "Not really."

"Nothing ever happened with Mr. Creffield that seemed to you . . . wrong?"

"I don't know."

"You don't know?"

"No," I said, with a flash of anger. "How should I? I'm only seventeen. I'm not married. So no one's ever told me how things ought to be. Between a man and a woman, I mean."

"Hmm. That's exactly the point, Eva. You're not a woman yet. So there shouldn't have been *anything* between you and Mr. Creffield."

My cheeks flamed. He didn't understand. Joshua was not just any man.

"Let me ask you this, Eva. Do you know how babies are begun?"

"Yes," I said, ashamed that I did know.

"Well, then?"

"Well then what?"

"Did that happen to you?"

I hesitated. "Is that the criminal thing?"

"Well, I think that's quite obvious, isn't it?"

"Is it? How can the thing that starts babies be criminal?"

Mr. Gardner sighed deeply. "My dear, in this case, it would be criminal because you're a child. It would be criminal if he forced you. Did he?"

I glanced at the door. What if I bolted? How far would I get?

"It might interest you to know, Eva Mae, that Florence testified to me about this. She told me Mr. Creffield most definitely did take advantage of her."

"She did?"

He nodded. "So what is your answer, Eva Mae? Once and for all, did Mr. Creffield force you to have relations with him?"

Florence had told? I held back one more instant, stiff and tense. But what was the use of denying it any longer?

"I don't know," I cried helplessly. "Maybe. It

happened so fast. I don't remember agreeing, but I didn't stop him either." My eyes welled with tears, my vision of Mr. Gardner blurred. "Was I supposed to stop him?"

He closed his eyes briefly. "You needn't worry about that, my dear," he said gently. "This is his crime, not yours." He let out a long sigh. "All right, then." He took a breath. "Tell me when. And where."

"Last summer," I whispered.

"I'm sorry, my dear. I can't hear you."

"Last summer," I said. "On the island."

And then I gave him the details he required, but only the barest of them, answering what he asked and no more. I didn't try to explain what he couldn't possibly understand, that somehow my believing Joshua's story about holy rituals had made the whole thing different.

When we'd finished with my pitiful little confession, Mr. Gardner looked at me with the kindliest, saddest eyes.

"Did you not understand, Eva Mae, that a very great wrong was done to you?"

Was it? I suppose so, but now I could only hang my head, shame burning my cheeks. For what answer could I make? That I'd had no understanding of such things? That no one warned me? That nothing happened to me that hadn't happened to the others too, and none of them cried foul? That it was all because I'd hoped to be Second Mother, something beautiful and holy?

Looking back, I'm glad Mr. Gardner was the one to first hear this from me. My father would receive the report soon enough, but I would be spared the witnessing of it—his first anguished rage at learning the truth.

The truth that was even harder to admit to myself than to Mr. Gardner.

That in the eyes of the world, I was a ruined girl.

HOLY ROLLER GOES TO INSANE ASYLUM

Mrs. O. V. Hurt, of Corvallis, Taken to Salem by Her Husband Yesterday Afternoon.

COMMITTED FROM CORVALLIS

O. V. Hurt, of Corvallis, who some months ago received a great deal of unpleasant notoriety as a result of the conversion of his wife, son, and daughters to Creffieldism, the sect known as the "Holy Rollers," was in the city yesterday afternoon on his way to Salem where he placed his wife in the asylum for treatment, she having yesterday afternoon been committed to that institution by the Benton County court. Mrs. Hurt, who appears as an intelligent woman before her conversion to Creffieldism, was olad much as were the young women who were sent to the asylum from Corvallis some time ago, and she like them, wore her hair loose and down her back. Mr. Hurt hopes that his wife, the mother of his children, will soon recover from her insanity, for he firmly believes her mind is deranged.

Mr. Hurt has been sorely tried by the craze that settled over some Corvallis families as the result of the coming of Creffield ...

The Albany Herald, June 30, 1904

*T*he only letters allowed me were from my father, who wrote pleasant missives full of nothing but good cheer about a world that seemed so far away. Why, they'd brought a merry-go-round to town and parked it down on the flats! People were gathering there every evening and having a most enjoyable time! He certainly hoped I'd be able to come home before they took it away!

Even when he wrote that he'd been forced to put Mama in the insane asylum, he managed a certain optimistic tone, recommending I try thinking of it as merely a pleasant hospital.

I sat on my iron bed, reading this terrible news spelled out in his firm and confident handwriting. Was it possible Mama truly *had* gone insane? Had we all? When people spoke of someone losing her mind, is this what they meant? This state of foggy numbness? Surely Mama had more reason to be disturbed than any of us, caught as she'd been between Papa, watching her every minute, forever threatening her with the asylum, and Joshua, hiding under the house, depending on her for food.

Joshua.

My breath caught. Papa's letter fell to my lap. Joshua would be left under the house now, with no one to bring food. Would he starve? Run away?

What was I even hoping for?

Late in the evening in the dormitory, I would lie on my bed and stare at the bare lightbulb dangling from its long cord. Sometimes I'd listen to the other girls talking. They weren't orphans, for the most part. Two were here to bear babes they wouldn't be allowed to keep. Others hinted of sick, defeated mothers with too many children, unemployed fathers who boxed their ears in drunken rages.

My home had been a haven in comparison, I realized. At least my home the way it had been before Joshua. How long ago that seemed, the time when he wasn't lodged in my mind, possessing my every thought.

Sometimes I considered running away, but trying it seemed useless. They watched us like hawks, and even if they did make Boys' and Girls' look like a regular house, with roses around the outside and all, everyone knew it was locked up tight enough at night. If it weren't, they'd never have been able to keep Esther three months.

One evening I got off my bed and walked over to stand at the window. It was summer, and the air smelled sweet. I looked down at the lawn two stories below and thought about escape. Could I throw down a rope of knotted sheets? Even if I landed safely, though, then what? I wouldn't know which direction to run. The train trip here with my father was a blur, and I had no idea which streetcar line we'd ridden from Union Station. I knew only that I was somewhere in the big city of Portland.

"Psst!"

I turned around and found the upturned face of one of the little girls. Millie, her name was. I believe she was about eight.

"What're you doing?" she asked.

"Just looking."

"Oh." She hesitated a moment. "Eva Mae? I think your hair's so pretty. But how come you always leave it loose?"

I shrugged. "Habit, I guess." Somehow I couldn't see trying to explain how Joshua had convinced us anything else was a sin.

"Want me to plait it for you?" Her little face looked so hopeful. "I'm pretty good at it, see?" She held out her own little bits of braid.

I smiled. And it was the oddest thing, that smile. Because I noticed it. You don't notice your own smiles, I wouldn't think, unless you haven't smiled in months and then your first one fair cracks your cheeks with the strangeness of it.

"All right then." I perched on the edge of her bed. "Mind you do mine as pretty as yours, though."

It was not unpleasant, letting her comb and tug and plait. Perhaps some order restored to my person, I thought, would help return order to my mind.

So when exactly did my cure commence? Was it that first bite of food? Confessing to Mr. Gardner? Letting Millie braid my hair?

Maybe it was the ice cream.

For the Fourth of July several rich charity ladies donated ice cream and firecrackers to the Boys' and Girls' Aid so we might have a bit of a celebration, a party spread out on the lawns, complete with red, white, and blue bunting draped around the tables. The children looked so sweet, dressed up in their best mended and carefully pressed hand-me-down outfits, waving their tiny flags. The fog in my mind seemed to be lifting, and for a while at least, the world looked vivid, full of color again. And, oh, I'd forgotten how good ice cream tastes!

I might also give credit for the hastening of my mind's clearing to little Millie herself, who'd taken to trailing me around as if I were her big sister.

I had become accustomed to lying to grown-ups, but it was different with Millie. When she looked at me the way she did, so trusting, I had to actually stop and think about what I said. The practiced answers didn't spring so automatically to my lips.

"Eva?" she said, seated there beside me on the lawn that day. "Did your papa used to hit you?"

"Oh, no!" I said, disturbed at the matter-of-fact way she could mention such a thing. "No, my father is a very kind man."

"Why did you have to come here, then? Is it about that Holy Roller thing the big girls were talking about?"

"Millie, they talked about that in front of you?"

She nodded. "Well, yes, my father was worried. About my religious beliefs."

"God and Jesus and such?"

I nodded.

"Well, what *do* you believe?"

I looked at her. Such a simple question. And those big eyes of hers, wide and waiting. At that moment it struck me—she thought I understood about things. Just because I was a few years older, she thought I knew.

Just like I'd always thought Maud knew.

"Eva?" Millie prompted me.

"Well," I said, "I believed . . ." I believed this beautiful world was going to end any minute? I believed a man who called himself Joshua had all the answers and every other person on earth who didn't believe in him was doomed? Even innocent little children like Millie here? We imagined we were the only two dozen in the whole world who would be saved?

Wait. No. We couldn't have believed that, could we?

I watched the children enjoying their ice cream.

It didn't seem right, now.

I looked at Millie. "I'm sorry, pet. I hardly under-stand it myself."

How could I explain that I'd been living with a man inside my head who watched over me every moment, directing my thoughts, passing a terrifying judgment on every word I spoke?

In the downstairs parlor at Boys' and Girls' they kept a big piano, and once in a while we'd hear someone play-ing very nicely.

That evening I was upstairs, standing at the window again, looking out at the fir trees silhouetted against the magenta sky, when the strains of a familiar song came drifting up. "The Last Rose of Summer."

In a rush of longing I remembered my own sweet home, my family, and especially my papa, who always liked hearing me play that piece so much. I burst into tears and had the homesick cry of my life, not caring who saw me.

Alarmed, Millie ran for the matron.

"Oh, Mrs. Graham," I said when she bustled in. "I want to go home. I'm cured, truly. I'm not a believer anymore, I promise."

That very night I began a campaign of letters to my father, swearing I'd given up the religion and begging him to come get me.

All I wanted was to go home.

One Sunday three weeks later, at the end of July, I was called down to the parlor. There stood my father, hat in hand.

"Papa!" I cried, and ran into his arms, burying my face against his shoulder. The ferocity of my embrace must have startled him, but I was desperate to blot out the voice of Joshua in my head, the voice that even at that moment was condemning me for such a show of misplaced affection.

"Pack your bags, my dear. I'm taking you home."

And on the train, Papa told me what the whole world already knew, that Joshua had been discovered under our house and was now in the Multnomah County jail in Portland.

Good, I thought. He's out of our house.

Now, God help me, if I could only get him out of my mind.

CHAPTER FIFTEEN

Clearly my father had been given an intimate report on my confession to Mr. Gardner.

"Are you all right, my dear?" he asked at least a half dozen times on the train ride. "Truly?" Somehow I knew he was not just wondering if I needed a sandwich from the dining car.

I felt conscious of him watching me with the tenderest looks as I climbed the front steps upon our arrival home. I still remember him standing there, circling his hat in his hands. I thought then his look was one of pity; I now understand it was more his own shame. How deeply it must have wounded him to learn what had befallen the daughter he'd been honor bound to protect.

But in those first days home, of greater concern to me than my so-called ruination was the simple reclaiming of my poor bewildered mind. Would I ever be able to think straight again? Regain that cheerfully trusting view of life I'd known before? Would I ever be able to make my own decisions? For a puppet whose strings are cut will fall in a heap, a puppet still. I had to learn to rise and walk on my own.

I began by simply putting one foot in front of the other, never looking beyond the task at hand.

At first the place felt terribly empty without the others. At Boys' and Girls' I had been surrounded by strangers. The absence of my mother and my sister was only in keeping with the disjointed nature of that interlude. But here I seemed to encounter their shadows around every corner. And to think of them was to picture them locked in the asylum.

To banish those fearful visions, I prescribed for myself the work cure, reestablishing the time-honored schedule of washing on Monday, ironing on Tuesday, right through to baking on Saturday. The structure I'd cast off before I now gladly embraced. To rise in the morning with the assumption that the world would continue and therefore dishes must be washed and floors swept—this was a habit I had to learn anew.

The first time I walked into town alone for some canning supplies, people stared at me. Just how crazy is she? I could almost see them thinking. How wayward does a girl have to be to wind up in a home for wayward girls? Yet I think I must have looked normal enough, wearing every prescribed layer of clothing from my corset on out, a beribboned straw hat over my properly pinned-up hair. What had constricted me before now felt like protective armor. And if my mind wasn't entirely back to normal, if I still had the odd turn of thought about the clouds cracking open with the blinding flash of Armageddon, well, who was to know?

Since our furnishings had been pared back to almost nothing in our quest for simplicity, Papa encouraged me to send for a few things from the Sears, Roebuck catalogue. He approved my rehanging of pictures on the walls. He urged the purchase of new lace curtains and a beautiful, rose-painted lamp, finding comfort, I think, in any evidence I had turned away from practices associated with Joshua Creffield. Indeed, had I the heart for it, I believe I could have refurnished our home in the grandest of styles, so relieved was he to believe me returned to normal, so grateful to have some order in the house again.

In truth, I took little joy in any of it, even when he had a telephone put in and explained how I could, as lady of the house, call stores around town with my orders. This was the modern way everyone was doing it now, he said.

"Do be careful what you talk about on the telephone, though, my dear," he warned me. "They say people have taken to amusing themselves by listening in on the party lines."

I soon discovered the truth of this when I picked up the receiver one morning and heard Joshua's name spoken. My whole body jerked, torched aflame. Paralyzed, I stood there listening as some woman enjoyed herself recounting to at least two enthralled listeners the story of Joshua's dreadful condition when he'd been pulled from under our house, pale and hairy and so wretchedly weak he could hardly stand up. And how his eyes had shone from the darkness of his jail cell with the queerest light. . . .

I hung up, trembling.

For me, on the subject of Joshua, there was only shame and disquiet. Shame to have betrayed him; shame to have followed him in the first place. Thinking about him at all made me extremely nervous, for then I would hear his voice and see his eyes and feel his condemnation at the life I was leading now.

I would have preferred ignoring altogether the news of his trial that September. Papa insisted, however, on reading about it to me from the newspapers, heaping up the damning evidence as if to bolster me against changing my mind and reverting to the faith.

Joshua was now putting it out that he was the reincarnation of Elijah. In court he admitted to the adultery with Aunt Nell, claimed it was God's will, and took every opportunity the judge afforded to quote scripture and make speeches about being misunderstood.

The jury took a mere fifteen minutes to find Joshua guilty, and he was given the maximum sentence of two years in the Oregon State Penitentiary in Salem.

Finally, with Joshua put in prison and no longer the subject of newspaper articles, the time alone with my father began to take on a quality of healing simplicity. I did not have to argue with anyone. I did not have to justify myself. All I had to do was look after my father's needs, and in so doing, perhaps make a start at repaying him for the grief I'd caused.

One evening, about the time the maples were going gold along the river, I was playing "The Last Rose of Summer" on the piano when I heard Papa in the doorway behind me. I turned.

"Papa, what is it?" I asked, rising in alarm at the expression on his face. "Bad news?"

"No, no," he said, motioning me back down. "Don't stop. I'm just—" He blinked off a tear. "I'm just so grateful to have at least *one* back again."

"Oh, Papa, don't be sad." I rose and went to him, laying my head on his chest. "It won't be long before the others come home too."

He nodded, putting his arms around me. "And by God, when they do, we won't ever have to talk about any of this again." His voice gathered strength. "I swear, it'll be as if none of it ever happened."

Desperate to believe him, I pulled back and gave him the smile he wanted.

AN ENDED CHAPTER

All the Creffield Victims Restored, and All at Home—
Hypnotism did it.

Mrs. Frank Hurt and Miss Attie Bray arrived Thursday from Salem and are now at the Hurt home in this city. All the members of the family are again at the fireside, fully restored in mind, and fast regaining bodily strength. Almost the unanimous testimony of each is that in the present reunion there is apparent wakening from a long nightmare, a fact that confirms the view that many have long held, that it was hypnotic influence that was responsible for manifestations of religious zeal during recent months. Those in the best position to know are fully convinced this is the correct theory, and those who passed under its influence were helpless under the will of a mind that in some way held control of their acts. Such things be in the world, and it is not of the remarkable that the influence suggested is responsible for all that has transpired.

Of those recently at Salem, Miss Sophia Hartley is the only one left at the hospital, and she is expected home before a very long time. All of the others are fully restored, and the end of the unfortunate chapter is here.

The Corvallis Times, December 10, 1904

Mama and Maud and Attie came home from the asylum looking stunned and tentative, and who could blame them? If you've felt yourself to be center stage in a great drama, a thrilling story which might, on any given day, climax with your ascension into the clouds, it's not so easy to return to your old place in the real world.

If Joshua wasn't a true prophet—and everyone now reluctantly admitted he wasn't—then there was nothing special about us either. At best we were simply a bunch of foolish girls who'd prided ourselves in our own righteousness. At worst we were ruined women, social outcasts.

The winter sky descended upon us and the rivers rose up, and out any window our gazes were met with naught but unrelieved gray. Watching the raindrops slide down the pane, the notion that the people of Corvallis had been right all along was not a particularly pleasant one to accept.

Attie returned to service at the Kline house. I rarely

saw her and found myself making no effort to do so, for her sad face reminded me of too much I wanted to forget.

Frank and Mollie moved to Seattle.

With Joshua now safely behind bars, Esther, we heard, had been allowed by her brothers back to Oregon City, where she was living with the Seeley sisters.

Maud suffered the most during this time, I think. The man locked in the penitentiary was still her husband, after all. While Mama slowly improved and helped me look after things, Maud did nothing but brood and eat, consuming huge meals with the driving force of misery behind her until her girth began to expand alarmingly.

"What does it matter?" she said every time she had to let her waistbands out yet again.

One day in the spring she confided that Papa was pressuring her to divorce Joshua.

"As if my marriage vows meant nothing to me," she said bitterly. "Oh, Eva, do you think I should? Ask for a divorce?"

I was surprised and strangely touched—Maud asking advice from *me*. Caring what *I* thought.

That summer she let Papa help her file the papers. She regretted the marriage, she said. She just hoped God would forgive her and know that she'd only been trying to find her path as a true Christian.

After that we never brought it up again, relying on

what I'd come to think of as our family motto: Don't talk about it and it didn't happen.

That hardly stopped the neighbors, of course, from discussing "the unfortunate episode." That's what they oh-so-politely called it on the party line. But as the months passed, the gossip died down. People couldn't talk about us forever, after all, not when we were adding nothing new to the story.

By New Year's 1906, I regarded the dark nightmare as part of the past and felt that Maud and I could once again walk the streets of Corvallis without hanging our heads and fixing our eyes on the boardwalk before us.

CHAPTER SEVENTEEN

*A*nd then, on a raw day in early spring, shortly after Mama had left us to walk into town, I opened the front door and got a shock.

"Esther!"

"Well," she huffed, "I thought your mother would never leave the house."

I just stood there, stunned. Esther, after all this time, talking as if we might have spoken only yesterday.

"Listen," she said. "I have messages from Joshua."

I stared at her. "Joshua?"

"He's been released from prison early." A slow smile curved her lips. "Good behavior."

"But Esther," I said, horrified. "That's over."

"Oh, no it isn't." She held out a letter. "This is for you."

No, I was thinking even as I felt her pressing the envelope into my hand. No, this can't be happening.

"Esther!" It was Maud, pushing me aside to draw Esther in and close the door.

"Joshua's in California," Esther said, low and

intense. "He's been writing to us at the Seeleys and we're hand delivering the letters to everyone else. We know your father watches the mail. And I wasn't sure about your mother. People have been saying she's given up Joshua."

"But, we all have," I said uncertainly, looking at Maud.

My sister, however, had eyes only for my letter. "Isn't there one for me?"

"Maud!" I couldn't believe it. The last time there'd been any discussion of Joshua, she'd voiced nothing but regret.

"No letter," Esther said. "But a very important personal message." She lowered her voice. "He wants you to marry him again."

Maud's hands flew to her cheeks.

"He wants you to come to Seattle."

"God in heaven," Maud said.

"But we gave him up," I repeated desperately.

Esther raised her eyebrows at Maud. "Joshua's not going to be pleased to hear about *her*, is he?"

"Never mind," Maud said breathlessly. "Tell me more. Did he write this? That he wants to marry me again? Have you seen him?"

"I'll tell you everything," Esther said between her teeth, "if your little sister here will be still."

Oh, God, I thought, watching Maud. Her face was transformed, filled with light. It was *him*, inside her again, possessing her just like before.

"Maud, please," I said. "Remember what—"

"Don't you see what this means?" she cut me off. "He *does* honor his marriage vows. He has all along." She tilted her head and regarded Esther wistfully. "Oh, Esther, you're so . . ." She shook her head, humbled by Esther's slender loveliness. "I don't know why he doesn't want to marry *you.*"

Esther sighed as if perhaps she'd wondered about Joshua's choice too. "I'm still to be Second Mother, but it's you he wants for a wife."

I couldn't believe it. Couldn't believe they were talking like this. Just picking right up where they'd left off, as if the whole past year and a half had never happened.

"But Esther, look at me." Maud glanced down at her expanded waistline. "He wouldn't want me if he saw me now."

I grabbed her hands. "Maud! Didn't we all decide he was a *bad man*? He took advantage of us!"

"Will you be quiet!" Esther said, then she turned back to Maud. "Believe me, he wants you."

At this Maud's face went radiant again. Dreamily, she pulled her hands away from mine.

"Maud," I pleaded, still trying to reach her, "remember when you were even asking my advice what you should do? Whether you should divorce him? You didn't believe in him then, did you?"

"Get your coat, Maud," Esther said. "We're going for a walk. Obviously we can't discuss this in front of *her.*" She turned back and put her face close to mine. "And don't you dare breathe a word of this, do you hear?"

When Esther had steered Maud out, I took the letter up to our room. It was like a serpent in my hand. Should I burn it unread? Probably, yet something compelled me to open it.

My dear Eva Mae, it began, *You know you are mine and mine alone and thus it shall ever be. Soon we will be gathering the flock to establish our Eden. I feel the End is very near and it is of the utmost importance that we all be together on that most awesome and glorious day. So delay not in your preparations and await my message that the time has come for you to leave the vile and the unholy and join us . . .*

And so it continued, pages and pages. In his release from prison, he said, he'd been resurrected. He had been to hell and was now truly Christ come again, and God would smite anyone who did not obey his word.

I have found the people of San Francisco no better than the infidels of Corvallis or Seattle, and God has therefore commanded me to lay a great curse upon them all. Their cities will crumble to rubble and be consumed by the flames of their own iniquity. Death will call upon them, cutting them down like a scythe through the wheat. Only those who turn their backs on sin and believe in me shall be saved. . . .

I stared at the letter, panicked. Reading the words, I could hear his voice, I could see his eyes again, boring into me. I wished he were dead. I did! Just knowing he was out there, trying to lure us all back . . . Oh, God, he was like a whirlpool, sucking us in, dragging us down.

Would everyone leap back in? Had they all secretly remained loyal to him? But no, they would have told me. Wouldn't they?

But wait. Who said I had to go along with everyone else? I'd been but a child when this began. Three years ago, I'd followed Maud and the others with little questioning. Hadn't I grown up since then? I wouldn't allow it! I simply would not be possessed!

I jumped to my feet. I tore the letter into the tiniest bits and threw them away.

"Oh, Maud, please tell me you're not going," I begged when she returned from her walk with Esther. "Don't leave me!"

"Then you come too," she said simply.

"Maud! If we both ran away? That would break Papa's heart."

Her lips pressed together. "That's all you care about, isn't it? Poor Papa. Well what about me, Eva? What have I got here? Nothing. And Joshua does love me. Maybe you're too young to understand, but any ordinary man would choose Esther over me in a minute."

"Stop saying that!"

"But that's the very thing that proves it. Joshua choosing me shows he's *not* ordinary. This convinces me more than ever that he truly is a man of God. And as the Bible says, 'he who would serve me, must follow me.'"

"But Maud, that was *Jesus* saying that. Joshua is not Jesus!"

She looked at me. "Are you so sure?"

I burst out crying. "Don't, Maud. Don't talk like that. You're scaring me. I can't stand to go back to the way it was!"

Should I tell Papa? *Joshua wants us back.* Oh, I shuddered just thinking it. Imagine my father's reaction if I actually said those words out loud!

But did I owe him a warning?

Before I could even decide, Maud got on the train for Seattle with our parents' blessing, having told them she wanted to go help Frank and Mollie with their new baby.

In no time at all, word came back from Seattle: Maud had remarried Joshua.

Papa was livid. "How *could* she?" he kept saying, and finally he turned to me. "And now I suppose you'll go running off too?"

"No, Papa! No, truly."

And God be my witness, when I said that, I meant it.

Easter morning dawned bright and fair. Alone, I sat erect in a hard wooden pew at the Episcopal church, where I had determined to come as if to demonstrate to my father my independence of thought.

He had offered to buy me a new hat for the occasion, but I had declined. Church meant more to me now than an excuse to dress up. As the light streamed through the arched windows upon the fern-and-lily-banked altar, we rose to sing of the true Christ, and I felt the spirit of the words vibrate through my very being.

Tis the spring of souls today: Christ hath burst His prison
From the frost and gloom of death, light and life have risen.
All the winter of our sins, long and dark is flying
From His light, to whom we give thanks and praise undying.

Standing there with my hymn book, for just that moment, I felt safe. I felt surrounded by the light that would protect me from the darkness of Joshua. The voices lifted in this hymn of praise blocked Joshua's voice in my head. He was the valley of the shadow I had passed through, and I would never go back. I didn't dare even *look* back for fear of the deathly power of his very eyes.

I was sorry when the service ended, almost frightened when the last organ notes faded. Outside I watched this good congregation of people setting out for their homes and their Easter dinners. Those I recognized even smiled and nodded at me.

They seemed like such happy, right-thinking people. And *they* had never believed Joshua. *They* weren't afraid the world might end. I wanted to be like them. I wanted to be a girl who didn't have the voice of Joshua in her head.

I wanted to throw myself at them, beg them to hold onto me and keep me from slipping away.

Instead I just stood there, watching the birds swoop around the church's chimneys, landing on the wings of those lovely stone angels.

CHAPTER EIGHTEEN

The next day Mama sent me into town for laundry soap, a box of clothespins, and a length of line. I was to look for a new rug beater too. She said we couldn't do anything about Maud, but spring cleaning was still a business we could master.

I was passing Hode's Groceries when Attie swooped by, looping her arm through mine.

"I'm so glad I caught you," she said. "Listen. This is extremely important. I have a message from Joshua. He's sent word we're to gather at the coast. The plan is to take up government land for our colony. I'm leaving tomorrow."

"Attie!"

"Yes, I know," she said, misunderstanding my alarm. "I almost had to go without talking to you, but I was afraid to telephone or come to the house. Now. Everyone's traveling on different days, so as not to arouse too much suspicion. You ought to come, say, Wednesday."

"But—"

"But, what?" she demanded.

"Attie." My voice quavered. "We disavowed him."

She looked away, her expression pained. "Faith is a mysterious thing, Eva. We've been force-fed nothing but lies about Joshua all this time. Anyone might break down. Yet the very minute I received his message—" She snapped her fingers. "Just like that, I knew the truth, as if I'd never forgotten it. I knew I was still willing to follow him anywhere."

She sounded so sure.

"And the End signs are all around us. Right there in the newspapers. Famines, pestilence, earthquakes."

Only Friday we'd read of thousands dying in an eruption of Mount Vesuvius. . . .

"So," she said, "everyone's coming. This is it, Eva— the End Time. You've heard about Joshua's curse on the cities, haven't you? The only place that'll be safe is our new Eden."

My stomach turned. The visions she was conjuring . . .

"As far as your mother, pet, I'm sorry, but we can't take her. We can't even tell her. Believe me, we've discussed it at length. But Maud says your father has too much control over her now. If she heard about this it would go straight to him, and he'd probably lock *you* up. You wouldn't be able to get away."

My heart was pounding now. What if only half of what she said was true?

"So, take the one forty-five train," she went on. "It

gets into Yaquina at six. We'll be meeting each train, taking people over to the camp place. Probably down by Alsea Bay." She gripped my shoulders, made me look at her. "I'll see you in Yaquina, Eva. Wednesday."

I turned and started home, then remembered my errands. I couldn't go back empty-handed. Retracing my steps, I went into the hardware store and asked for clothespins.

"Do you want the regular ones, Miss Hurt? Or the new?"

"What?"

"This new model with the spring is supposed to be easier to get off your line when it freezes."

I must have been staring like an idiot. If the world was ending, why was I buying clothespins?

Oh, God, I had never expected to have anything to do with Joshua again. But my favorite cousin . . . my only sister . . . all my friends . . . the only people on earth who shared with me what we'd all been through. I was going to be left behind!

Finishing my purchases, I went home and delivered them to my mother, who was stationed at the back porch washtub. Then I climbed the stairs and threw myself across my bed, utterly sick.

Could Attie be right? No! I wouldn't believe it. And it was so unfair! Hadn't we all agreed on this? And now they had all changed without warning.

But think, I told myself. Think straight. Don't let yourself be fooled. You *know* what's right. You don't have to let Joshua lay hold on you again.

No matter what I told myself, though, there was no denying I was completely unnerved. My usually hearty appetite failed me, and I could hardly sleep that night as I anguished over the dilemma. True, I had a right to make up my own mind. On the other hand, who did I think I was to imagine myself smarter than all the rest of them put together? Could I really be the only one who was right?

The next night was no better. Even when I slept, I found no rest, for I dreamt of Joshua under the house again, his power rising to surround me, smother me in my bed. I woke with a start and couldn't go back to sleep. Indeed, I had already been staring wide eyed into the darkness for hours when the first bird chirped outside my window.

I came down the stairs feeling light-headed and anxious, yet determined.

I was right. I had decided in those brooding hours that Attie and the rest of them were wrong. Today was Wednesday, the day she had told me to come. Today my refusal to join the others would be made clear.

As I sat down to my breakfast porridge, the telephone rang in the hall and Mama answered.

"Mercy, how dreadful!" I heard her exclaim. "This morning?"

It sounded like the usual accident report being buzzed around the party lines: a runaway team overturning a wagon, a drowning in a spring-flooded tributary, an alarming new incident of typhoid. Sometimes I wondered about the wisdom of having a telephone. Often, it seemed, the new contrivance simply meant a swifter receipt of the latest bad news.

Mama kept murmuring sympathetically. Would she ever ring off and tell me what on earth had happened? I pushed aside my half-eaten breakfast, curious in spite of myself.

Finally she appeared in the doorway.

"What is it, Mama?"

"San Francisco," she said, hand pressed to her breast. "My goodness! They've had the most terrible earthquake."

I stood.

"They're saying hundreds of people are dead and the city is almost destroyed."

I sucked a great, head-tingling breath and crumpled to blackness.

CHAPTER NINETEEN

Good-bye to the muddy spring Willamette, good-bye to all the steepled churches, good-bye to the courthouse and The Flight of Time. My heart pounded as my boot heels knocked along on the boardwalk. Good-bye to these picket fences, tidy houses, and tree-lined streets. All would be rubble soon. Death and flames and contagion.

At the train station window I stepped up only at the last minute and bought my ticket for Yaquina. On the train — mercifully uncrowded — I slipped into a seat by the window. As we pulled away, I leaned my forehead against the glass and looked my last at Corvallis. I did not expect to see it ever again.

And yet the rushing thrill of the coming rapture overcame any grief. We were *not* just foolish girls! We *were* the Chosen Ones!

The train dove through deep-cut, fern-lined banks, then shot out across trestles where the ground dropped away beneath us. Alongside the tracks, I gazed into pale green rivers; above us, rags of torn clouds threaded through the ridge-top firs.

At the hamlet of Summit, we stopped in front of the store. The farm woman who boarded took the seat across the aisle from me. As the train pulled out, I felt her curious eyes upon me and turned away, bowing my head over clenched hands.

Every other person traveling on the train or standing at the stops along the way no doubt regarded this as an ordinary day. I, alone, prayed in simultaneous terror and jubilation, certain that never before had two such powerful emotions done battle so fiercely in one heart. Joshua was the true prophet, and I had betrayed him with my faithlessness. Now I was no more prepared for the rapture than those who had scoffed at him from the very beginning. But maybe he'd still take me! Maybe it wasn't too late and I too would wear the raiment of white.

I could hardly bear to look out at the sky, for fear of what I might see.

"And lo, there was a great earthquake; and the sun became black as sackcloth of hair; and the moon became as blood; And the stars of heaven fell unto the earth...."

"Are you all right, dearie?" It was the woman across the aisle. "You look a bit peaked."

I managed a weak smile.

"Hungry? I've got some nice sourdough biscuits here." She tapped the wicker hamper she carried.

I shook my head no.

On and on we went, mile after mile, farther from home. I had made this trip a half dozen times with my family on summer excursions, but seen with the knowledge of imminent doom, the beauty of the fields and forests made my heart ache. Every newly unfurled bloom seemed suffused with such tragic innocence. Yet the next moment I'd be filled with exultation, remembering that the glory of the bright new Kingdom of God would surely surpass any such common sights as I had loved in this life.

We were on the coast side of the mountains now, following the Yaquina as it gathered its flow from the rushing creeks, winding through the white snags of an old burn. Here and there, we passed a little stump farm carved from the forest, a lone house in a clearing, the crimson flash of a flowering quince. In front of one cottage, a child on a fence perch waved at me.

At Elk City the river began to widen as the train chugged down onto the tidal flats. As it rounded a bend, the port of Toledo came into view. The next stop would be Yaquina City, the end of the line.

The end of the line. The end of the world. I was riding a train to the end of the world.

CHAPTER TWENTY

*A*t the wharf-side Yaquina station Attie met me as promised, then ushered me up the boardwalk to a big clapboard hotel. They'd taken rooms, she said, just until everyone else arrived. So far only Frank and Mollie were there.

When I came in, Mollie was nursing her four-month-old baby, my new niece. I smiled shyly, and little Ruthie's eye rolled in my direction. She fell away from the breast and grinned milkily at me.

"Oh, Mollie, she's a love," I said, a fresh wave of sadness washing over me. To think I would never have a baby of my own. Not now, with time itself running out.

"I hope you got away without telling Pop every last little thing," Frank said.

"I didn't tell him anything," I insisted. "Mama either."

It hadn't been easy. When I blacked out, Mama had brought me round with smelling salts and put me to bed, calling my condition a touch of the vapors. I'd had to lie there all morning rigid with fear, waiting for a chance to bolt for the one o'clock train.

And now, here I was. I felt as if I'd been raptured already, so swift was the shift from my old life to the new. And soon the Brides of Christ would all be together again. I could hardly believe it was really happening.

Late Saturday afternoon the door burst open and I jumped up, faint with fear and light-headed again from our reinstated regimen of scanty food and constant prayer.

Maud came huffing in, struggling with luggage and a number of paper-wrapped bundles.

"Maud!" I cried, rushing forth. We had but an instant to embrace, then pull back and look at each other. Oh, how worn and worried my poor sister looked! I tried to hide my dismay at the shabby state of her skirt and jacket.

"Eva," she said. "I'm so glad you've come."

I nodded, hoping she'd forgotten, or at least forgiven me, for arguing against this.

Then, a sudden hush. *He* must be here.

Slowly, I turned.

Joshua. He looked the same as ever, his features as handsome, his presence as compelling. His eyes locked on mine, holding me. I was the one at this moment. I was the one he hadn't seen in the longest time.

"Eva Mae." He held out his arms. "Come."

Unsteadily, I walked toward him, eyes downcast in fear, conscious of the others watching me. Did he know of my betrayal?

"Glory to God," he said as his arms went round me. "Glory to God for giving us this girl, for bringing her to us in this hour of peril."

Cheek against his chest, I let out a shuddering sigh. He wasn't angry. Oh, I wanted to cry with the relief of it. Whatever transgressions of faithlessness he might have detected in me, I had been forgiven.

Then, suddenly, the spell was broken and the others fell into an excited pandemonium, everyone speaking at once.

Sophie Hartley and her mother hadn't been on the train as planned, apparently, but her father, Lewis Hartley, was. After the arrival in Yaquina, he'd taken the ferry to Newport, threatening to come back with the sheriff.

"What can they arrest you for?" Mollie asked Joshua. "You haven't done anything."

"He says I'm holding his wife and daughter against their will. That they were on the train when he got on, and I must have them somewhere."

Everyone looked at Joshua, waiting.

"Well, I don't know where they are! We never saw them."

Maud explained how they'd detoured around Corvallis, getting off the train at Airlie and cutting through Kings Valley in a hired buggy.

"We weren't about to risk going through Corvallis and rousing all those lunatics," she said. "Not while we still have members there who have to escape."

Joshua crisscrossed the room, repeatedly glancing out the window.

"Shall we pray?" Attie asked.

"No," Joshua said. "I mean, yes, go ahead." But only a moment later he whirled from the window, interrupting our incantations. "God has spoken. We must leave. Right now. We'll go down to the camp."

"But what about the others?" Attie asked timidly.

"They'll find us. God will show them the way."

We gathered up what little we had to take with us—the baby, of course, a few satchels, and the mysterious bundles. We hurried downstairs to the landing where we milled around as the ferry docked. The sky had cleared and the sun was about to set. As soon as we'd boarded, Joshua turned to the ferryman.

"Shove off," he ordered.

The man raised an eyebrow. "Like to give it a few minutes, case anyone else comes. Last run of the day and all."

Joshua eyed the Newport ferry approaching and pulled out more money. "Go now."

And then, on the other ferry, we saw a man causing a stir, motioning his fellow passengers back.

"It's Lewis Hartley!" Maud cried. "He's got a gun!"

Joshua collared the ferryman. "For the love of God, man, now!"

Startled, the ferryman complied. Our craft began to move.

We were only a few yards from shore when, on the other ferry, Mr. Hartley struck a stance and aimed his revolver. We screamed in chorus and fell to the deck, expecting any instant the gun's report.

Nothing. No bang. Only our own muffled whimperings of fear.

Cautiously, I lifted my head. Joshua still stood. He threw back his head and laughed.

"You see!" His voice boomed clear and strong across the water. "No mortal man can kill me."

We all struggled up in a mixture of weeping and laughing relief.

"You dare to smite the Savior!" he shouted, pointing in condemnation. "God will smite *you*!"

Our cries of jubilation rose as Mr. Hartley, receding behind us, glared at the gun in his hand, the gun that had betrayed him, the gun that had proven Joshua to be what we had awaited so long — the Second Christ.

CHAPTER TWENTY-ONE

*A*t pink-streaked dawn, aching and stiff after our night in the shack serving as the South Beach transfer station, we boarded the stage wagon that would take us the fifteen miles down the beach to the next bay.

"What are these, anyway?" I whispered to Maud, referring to the paper-wrapped packages we loaded.

"Shh!" She glanced around. "Joshua will explain later." Then she took a seat up front next to him.

I was relegated to the back, where I had to sit with two passengers not in our group. Because of them, the rest of us didn't speak during the trip.

First, a bumpy ride over a wooden corduroy road took us out to the beach. Oh, the beautiful ocean! A fair prospect that took my breath away. The frothing white waves had a biblical look to them, and the cliffs and vast expanse of sea and sky did seem a fit backdrop for the dramatic climax Joshua had promised.

As the wind scudded clots of foam across the hard-packed sand and the wagon rolled briskly along, I wondered—had Corvallis fallen yet? Might my parents already be dead? I shuddered. I couldn't think of that. I must think only of the coming rapture, and these startling new proofs of Joshua's power. What a wonder! The way he'd stood against Mr. Hartley's gun. I fixed my eyes on Joshua's back, his shoulder rocking against Maud's.

At an outcropping of rocks jutting into the ocean, the driver urged the team up over a dirt road, where at one boggy spot we were even asked to get out and push. After another corduroy patch we joggled back down to the beach again and had to race the incoming tide, the waves hissing at the horses' hooves. Finally a hard pull over the sand spit at Alsea Bay.

"Stop here," Joshua directed the driver.

"You don't want to go to the landing?" the driver asked. "You need the ferry to get over to Waldport."

"This will do," Joshua said.

The driver looked around at the bleak landscape of sand and windblown trees. "Where you planning to stay?"

Joshua glared at him. "I fail to see where that's any concern of yours." A jerk of his chin signaled we should climb down out of the wagon. We followed him through a gap in the dunes to a wide stretch of beach facing the bay.

The sky was overcast; a stiff wind blew off the water.

Was this supposed to be Eden?

The sight of us looking hesitant and puzzled seemed to anger Joshua.

"Well, don't just stand there!" he cried. "Build a fire. A *big* fire."

We moved to do as we were bid, gathering drift-wood into a pile. As soon as the flames caught, we instinctively drew close to the warmth.

"You think this fire is for your comfort?" Joshua said. "That's the thinking of the ungodly. That's man's use for fire. God's purpose for fire is to purify." He tore open the first of the paper-wrapped bundles. "These are your new holy robes. Now throw off the old, the impure, and cast them into the fire."

"Our clothes?" Attie said in a small voice. I wasn't used to hearing her sound so timid.

"You heard me!"

Hands moved to buttons, but none too quickly. I was loathe to give up my jacket, for spring here by the ocean meant little in the way of relief from winter's chill.

"Hurry up!" Joshua cried, opening more bundles, throwing a garment at each of us.

Catching mine, I shook it out. A black dress.

Black.

What happened to the robes of white the Chosen Ones were to don at the End? Our raiment of light? These were wrappers, really—high-necked, button-fronted gowns made for wearing in a well-heated home. The satin fabric was thin and cheap, no protection at all against the cruel wind.

Stony faced, Maud threw her threadbare jacket on

the fire. Mollie too. I glanced at them and reluctantly dropped mine into the flames. I tried not to sniffle as I unhooked my skirt and eased it down over my hips, stripping to my chemise and drawers. Whether Joshua watched us undress, I don't know. I did not lift my own eyes until my black wrapper was buttoned up to my throat.

When I did, I saw that he and Frank had not donned any special attire. Neither were they burning their coats.

"Now your shoes," Joshua demanded, and we threw those onto the fire as well.

Next Joshua strode up to Attie and started yanking out her hairpins. Seeing what he was about, the rest of us made haste to undo our own hair before we had it done forcibly.

"There," he said when our tresses were loosed all around our shoulders and down to our waists. "Now you look like what you are—brides of the prophet, the light of the world, the future mothers of the New Eden."

I heard my own teeth chattering.

"Well, don't just stand there!" Joshua roared. "Build some shelters."

I looked around. "What shall we make them of?"

Joshua loomed over me. "God gives you a beach covered in driftwood and you have to ask what on earth you can use to make a shelter?"

"I'm sorry. I didn't think—"

"Bah!" He dismissed me with a disgusted wave, shaming me in front of the others.

Wrapping my arms around myself, I followed Attie to collect wood. This was not what I had expected. Visions of earthquake, fire, and flood had at least been dramatic. This was becoming miserable in such an ordinary way.

As soon as we had rigged the first shelter, Joshua slipped into it with Maud. Then we set about providing huts for ourselves. Frank left Mollie to finish theirs alone, saying he needed to catch the last ferry into Waldport for supplies. Attie and I made a little dugout in the sand, roofing it with driftwood. It would block the wind at least, even if the sand floor was damp and the roof would be no proof from the rain that now threatened. Then we huddled at the fire with Mollie and the baby.

"Do we have any food?" I asked.

"Not until Frank gets back," Mollie said. "And then we'll have to ration it. He didn't have money to buy much."

"Indians lived here for centuries," Attie reminded us. "They didn't have stores and they didn't farm, either. Why do you think Joshua chose this place? Because the ocean's full of fish and the woods are full of game. We can dig for clams too."

"Wouldn't we need a shovel?" Mollie said.

Attie didn't answer, and silence ensued. We stood in the smoke, hunched against the cold.

"Joshua scares me when he's angry," I said at last.

Attie put her arm around me. "I know, pet. But he can't help it. We have to remember what a burden he bears, caring for all of us, for all of our souls."

After a moment Mollie began a quavering hymn.

Attie and I joined her, but the sum of our voices was feeble and forlorn, lost on the wind.

$\mathscr{D}$ay by day our numbers grew.

The Seeleys arrived the next afternoon, Rose red faced and grim, Florence looking older, her childlike cheerfulness gone — dissipated, no doubt, by those long hours at the woolen mills.

Then the Hartleys stumbled into camp, Sophie thrilled to tell their tale of having slipped off the train in Blodgett when they realized Mr. Hartley was aboard. The remaining fifty miles they had traversed on foot, save for a wagon ride offered here and there.

Finally Esther made her appearance, cool, unruffled, fully prepared to once again don the mantle of Second Mother. Joshua himself came out of his shelter to warmly welcome her. When the furor died down and Joshua had once again retreated, she cast an accusing look at me.

"Your father," she said, "went up to Portland and filled my brother George full of lies about Joshua."

I blushed hotly. As if that were my fault. Anyway, he was Maud's father too. Why didn't Esther ever seem to blame *her*?

"Then George got the measles," Esther said, "and I think the fever went to his brain, because as soon as he could get out of bed, he was up tearing around. He went out to Nell's raving like a lunatic, swearing to hunt Joshua down.

"For all I know," she added, "he could have followed me here."

We looked over our shoulders apprehensively.

That night, Joshua gathered us at the fire for a solemn sermon.

"Stand all around me," he said. "Form a sacred circle of love." He took each of us in with his eyes, one at a time. "They want to kill me. You've all heard that. Just like they wanted to kill Christ. It's part of the prophecy. Did you know I'm just the age Jesus Christ was when he was crucified?"

Attie laid a hand over her breast. "Oh, Joshua—"

"No, Attie, this must be said. We all know they're out there with guns, but no matter what happens, you must promise to keep your faith. You may hear that I'm dead, but it won't be true. I'll come back to you. I'll be resurrected, just like Jesus."

Oh, his beautiful face in the firelight. His sad, suffering eyes. He made a picture at that moment I knew I'd remember forever.

"I'm putting my faith in each one of you to keep believing," he said. "Can you do that?"

"Oh, yes!" we instantly answered. "Joshua, yes." Who wouldn't feel privileged to be entrusted with such an important secret? Who didn't want to be deemed worthy, to pass the test of righteousness and purity and wear the crown of heaven?

The next morning a few of us were huddling around the fire when we were startled by a rough male voice.

"All right, where is he?"

We scrambled up as a figure emerged from the fog.

"Papa!" Sophie said, and spotting her father's rifle cried, "Don't you dare shoot that thing!"

"How *can* I?" Mr. Hartley complained as he approached. "The coward never comes out from behind you women. What? Is he hiding in that little hut there?"

"Joshua's not afraid of you," Mollie said, jiggling Ruthie, who'd begun fussing at the commotion. "You saw yourself he's proof against your bullets."

"Proof against my bullets as long as some fool sells me rimfire cartridges for a central fire gun. Where is he? Let him come out and try me again."

"Lewis!" cried Cora Hartley. "Don't! What good will it do for *you* to go to prison?"

"I don't care what happens to me," he said miserably, and for an instant I pitied him. The feeling was brief, though, lasting only until he hoisted his gun and started fingering the trigger again. "Somebody's got to put that man down and I'll tell you what, there's half a dozen of us fighting each other for the privilege." He looked at Esther. "Your brother'll be sorry to find out I got here first."

Esther sniffed. "But you got here too late. Joshua's gone."

Gone? I looked around. This was the first I'd heard of it. Some of the others seemed taken aback too. Not Attie, though. She leaned close to whisper to me that Maud had said to tell me good-bye.

So Maud was gone too. I sighed. Of course. She was his wife. She was only my sister.

It didn't surprise me they'd left, somehow, not when I recalled the odd note of finality in Joshua's voice when he'd spoken to us last night. Whatever the words, it had sounded like good-bye.

Mr. Hartley snorted with disgust. "Should have figured. Just like the sneaky little weasel to run off and leave you again."

"We're not *left*," Esther said. "It's all part of the plan. God's plan."

"That right?" He slowly scanned our campsite— the mean little shelters, our pitifully thin black dresses, the obvious lack of anything to eat. Then he shook his head. "Looks like a hell of a plan to me."

No one responded.

"All right then, have it your way," Mr. Hartley said to us. "But as for me and mine . . ." He seized Sophie and Mrs. Hartley by their wrists. "You're coming with me. I've got a wagon hired. And train tickets. We'll be home tonight."

My throat ached with unshed tears as I watched him drag them off toward the beach road. To think of Sophie sleeping in her own warm bed this very night.

Whereas I would never see home again.

First I had betrayed Joshua; then I had betrayed my own father by running off after promising I wouldn't.

Even if my faith in Joshua failed me, I'd have no right to go back, seeking forgiveness from Papa. Indeed, I deserved none.

I had chosen my course, burned my bridges. There was nothing for me but a blind stumbling forward to whatever my fate might be.

CHAPTER TWENTY-THREE

*N*ow our numbers began to diminish. Rose and Florence left, insisting they were in no way abandoning the faith. Frank decided to follow Joshua and Maud to Seattle, reporting that Joshua thought it best for Mollie to stay behind with the baby.

Finally Esther declared that God had once again spoken to her. "I'm directed to go into Waldport and remain there at the hotel for the time being."

I cut my eyes away. I wished God would tell me things like that.

She'd not been gone but a few hours when Aunt Nell arrived, deposited on the shore by a man in a rowboat.

I'll never forget Aunt Nell's ardent glow, her eager look as she scanned the camp, how quickly it disappeared when we reluctantly admitted Joshua was gone.

She had left her babies in Portland. She had ridden the train as far as a couple of pilfered dollars would take her, getting off just past Corvallis. From there she struggled over the muddy mountain road on foot until her heels were bleeding and bubbled with blisters.

But she was too late. And Joshua hadn't waited for her.

The next morning we were awakened by a small contingent of men from Waldport.

"You girls'll have to move on," one said. "We're God-fearing people in this town. We know what's going on with you Holy Rollers, and we're not going to tolerate this free-love business."

"Not going to have *our* daughters running out here," another added.

They offered to pay our ferry tolls providing we promised to keep moving, at which point Attie suggested her parents might shelter us if we could make it down to their ranch at Ten-Mile Creek.

And so began our final journey.

Abandoned brides of Eden.

What a cheerful sight we must have presented to the people of Waldport that gray morning as, barefoot, we came up the wooden gangplank from the ferry dock and traipsed the sandy main street, a bedraggled band in widow's weeds.

How my mouth watered at the smells of hot cooked food wafting out on the chimney smoke of those weatherworn cottages. Breakfast was being served, but not to us. For us, there was nothing but contempt on the faces that peered from behind checkered kitchen curtains.

In one window, though, I spied sympathy on the face of a girl my own age. Also, a look of wonderment in her eyes. I was not so different from her, I fancied she realized. How had I come to be dragging along in a torn black housedress, my long hair wildly tangled? Before we passed from each other's sight, some hand reached to yank her away.

"Don't mind them," Attie said. "Just remember who's going to be left behind at the Judgment."

With the tide still low enough, we picked our way around a sheltering point south of the village and came out upon a long stretch of beach, where the unchecked wind instantly began blasting sand into our eyes. While Mollie readjusted Ruthie's blankets, I shouted over the roar of wind and crashing breakers to Attie.

"How far is it?"

"They shall walk and not grow weary!" she cried over her shoulder, starting out again. "They shall mount up on wings of eagles!"

"Attie!" I wanted answers now, not scripture.

"Stop pestering!" she yelled. "It's not far." She pointed south to a steep cliff jutting into the ocean. "See that? The homestead's just on the other side."

My heart sank as I squinted into the distance. The headland was but a faint gray outline against the horizon.

"That's Cape Perpetua," she said, and a smile

tugged at the corners of her mouth. "Named for the martyr."

Heads bent to the wind, we trudged the long miles of hard-packed sand until finally the beach ended in a rock outcropping. There we followed a wagon road running up along the fence of a flat shelf of pasture, skirting the clustered cottages of Oceanview.

The Yachats River had no bridge or ferry, so we had to ford on foot. Attie insisted it was nothing, but I'm hard pressed to say which was worse — the numbing cold or the horror of wading through water up to our chins when we were none of us swimmers. Afterward, as we all stood drenched on the far bank, teeth chattering, she had the nerve to say, "Well, that was close, wasn't it?"

"Attie!" I stared through wet plastered strands of hair. "I thought you said you'd done this dozens of times!"

"Yes, but never in a spring flood like this! Now let's go along a little ways and make a camp. You didn't get those matches wet, did you, Eva?"

Most of the firewood was damp, but eventually we achieved a small blaze, around which we collapsed and slept, our stomachs gnawing with hunger. It hardly seemed possible, but truly, for discomfort and misery, every night was turning out worse than the last.

In the morning we set out again on a horse path that traversed the grassy, windswept flanks of the mountains. To the right, far below, furious white waves pounded the rocks. Here and there the path wound downward to a creek where we picked our way across on dry stones or balanced on fallen timbers.

Around noon, mounting a rise, we came face-to-face with it: Cape Perpetua.

We stopped, struck silent with dismay. Up close, the promontory seemed even higher and more fearfully steep than it had from a distance.

I shook my head. "I don't even see where the trail could be."

"Oh, it's there," Attie assured us. "Don't worry. And it's really not all that frightening. Not if the wind isn't blowing hard."

No wonder Attie had declined to fully describe the Cape Perpetua trail in advance—nothing but a narrow track running high around the face of a steep rock cliff, a path hardly wide enough for a horse, never mind a wagon of any sort.

"Don't look down," she kept saying. "Just don't look down and it's not hard at all."

I saw Mollie dart a glance in the direction of her feet, then squeeze her eyes tight as she clutched Ruthie to her chest.

I too chanced a look.

Oh, heart-stopping sight.

One stumbling step and you'd be cartwheeling thousands of feet into a churning white cauldron. If there'd been the slightest bit of food in my stomach, here, I believe, is where I would have lost it.

Hearts pounding, knees trembling, we inched our way along.

At the highest precipice I stopped, shivering with fear, my nails dug into the scant growth of lichen on the rock cliff face. Slowly, carefully, I turned my head to look out across the blue-green ocean.

I drew a sharp breath. Held it.

The curve of the earth. You could actually see it.

I exhaled, breathing hard a few times as I took it in, this sweeping glimpse of majesty.

Then I shut my eyes. It was all too much. I was too small.

And how had I ever come to be here, clinging to the side of this mountain?

CHAPTER TWENTY-FOUR

After many weary hours tramping the rugged trail, we finally rounded a point and saw spread before us a plateau of green, where dairy cows grazed by a creek and chimney smoke rose from a wind-weathered house.

The Bray homestead. Shelter at last.

Stumbling down the last of the rocky incline, we could see in front of the house two boys chopping and stacking firewood. More of my Bray cousins, I supposed, grown from the toddlers I'd met just once. Spotting our straggling band, the taller one embedded his ax in the block and hurried up the porch steps. His brother followed, glancing back at us over his shoulder.

As we approached, my Aunt Georgianah appeared on the porch, flanked by the boys. She squinted at us in the distance for just an instant before a jolt of recognition sent her hurrying down the steps and across the yard, palms to her cheeks in alarm.

"Oh, Attie! Oh, my poor dears." How clearly our pitiful state reflected itself in her eyes. "Eva Mae! Oh, my Lord, and you've got the new baby with you?"

"I'll get Pa," one of the boys said.

"No!" Aunt Georgie jerked around in alarm. "He'll"—the boy was already gone—"find out soon enough," she finished lamely. Then she sighed. "Well, let's get you poor things inside by the stove. Don't you girls know everyone's been frantic, wondering what's become of you? Sarah and Vic are probably worried half to death."

We followed her into the kitchen, where the heavenly aroma of baking bread made me swoon. Attie addressed her mother's back as the older woman shoved a hunk of wood into the cookstove firebox.

"We need a place to stay, Ma." Aunt Georgie closed the cast-iron door. "Just until our Joshua returns."

Aunt Georgie flinched. Slowly she turned around. "You haven't heard?"

"Heard what?"

Silence. I braced myself against the table.

"He's dead, Attie."

Dead.

The room blurred; a noise in my head started from nothing and swelled to a roar like the ocean. Someone slipped to the floor in a faint. Aunt Nell.

"Don't believe it!" Attie warned. "Remember what Joshua said."

I heard her only as if from a great distance, for some thick fog had instantly shrouded me. I was

vaguely conscious of her pulling up Aunt Nell and
propping her in a chair. Then Attie turned back to her
mother, squaring her shoulders and swallowing hard.
"It just can't be true, that's all."

"It sure as hell *is* true." The fearsome Ira Bray
loomed in the doorway. My dull gaze rested on his huge
hands, flexed into fists. "Shot down like the dog he is
and I'll tell you, there's nobody around here shedding
tears over it either."

"This was up in Seattle." Aunt Georgie looked at
Aunt Nell. "It was your brother did it. Your brother
George."

George. Yes, Esther had warned of this half-crazed
brother of theirs.

"He can't be dead," Attie said. "Lewis Hartley tried
to shoot him, but the bullets just bounced off. We saw,
with our own eyes." She whirled to the rest of us.
"Didn't we?"

We looked at each other and nodded, wide eyed, as
if our having witnessed this must surely affect anything
that might happen later.

"None but the Lord could kill Joshua," Attie said.
"No matter what you say we'll never — "

"Now you listen to me." Her father took a menac-
ing step closer. "That so-called Joshua of yours is dead
and that's the end of it. Every man in the state wishes
he'd pulled the trigger himself." He looked at me.
"Maybe even that idiot father of yours."

"Ira!" Aunt Georgie said.

"I don't give a good goddamn! Everybody knows Vic Hurt is the biggest fool around."

No! I didn't want to hear it! I didn't want to hear any of this. I put my hands over my ears and shut my eyes, but Ira Bray kept aiming his tirade right at me.

"Did you know they want to give that Mitchell boy a gold medal? People lining up to reward him for what he done. Taking care of a big mess your father never should have let get started."

"All right." Attie swallowed hard. "Maybe it's true about Joshua being dead."

Dead? She was saying that? I looked at Attie. Did that mean it might really be true?

"He warned us all the time this might happen," Attie went on. "In fact, he prophesied it. But we can wait right here for him just the same."

Ira Bray stared at her. "What in the —"

"Because we know he'll be resurrected."

Aunt Georgie looked horrified.

"You idiots!" her father exploded. "What'll it take? You ought to be hauled right back to the asylum until you can think straight again! Every one of you!"

Mollie and I shrank back, but Attie stood up to him. "Only the faithful believed Christ would be resurrected too."

"Get out!" he roared. "I won't stand for that kind of crazy talk in my house!"

"But wait, Ira! The baby." Aunt Georgie's voice sounded small but determined. "That baby is kin."

"Kin. That don't seem to matter to them." He turned on Aunt Nell. "You! Smearing your husband's good name all over the country. Running off, getting the whole disgusting story printed in the papers, even your idiot good-bye note." He sneered, and his hand twitched like it itched to strike. "Your spiritual love! Why, if you were my wife, I'd—"

"Ira, stop, please," Aunt Georgie pleaded. "Can't you see they've been through enough? We could at least give them a decent meal."

"No! That just lets 'em keep acting crazy. Maybe if they get cold and hungry enough, they'll come to their senses. They promise to give up on this man, hell, then we'll feed 'em. We'll feed 'em a goddamn banquet."

Attie looked at her parents. She looked at us.

"Let's go," she said.

Mollie and Aunt Nell headed out. But dull animal instinct held me back. I wanted to stay where it was warm. My shoulders sagged. What was the use? What was the use of anything? I slumped against the wall and slid down.

Attie seized me by my shoulders and pulled me up. "Eva," she said between her teeth, "have faith." And with that she pushed me out the door into a blast of cold wind.

Banished, heads down, stomachs aching with hunger, we trudged behind Attie back up the path the way we'd come.

I was crying now. Crying in confusion and sorrow

and rage. He *was* dead, wasn't he? I'd seen the tears Attie was fighting. And she never cried. I thought of Joshua's face, his beautiful face. How could we stand it, to think we'd never see him again? But if he didn't come back, it would be because he was a liar, because he wasn't Christ come again, so we shouldn't be sorry. Was that right? *Was it?* God help me, I couldn't even think straight anymore.

One step after another I plodded up the trail. Oh, couldn't this please just be over?

And then, above the ocean's roar, we heard someone calling. It was Aunt Georgie, hurrying along behind with a flour sack of bread. Since I was at the end of the line, she held it out to me. Wiping my tears, I staggered toward her.

"No." Attie marched down and barred my way with an outstretched arm. "We won't take it."

"But, Attie —"

"It would be a sin to eat bread baked in that poison air."

A keening whimper escaped me. Our hearts were broken. Wasn't that enough? Did we have to starve as well, just to prove something? And prove what?

Mollie shifted Ruthie in her arms.

We stood, wind whipping around us, waiting to see who might make the next move. I was as surprised as anyone to find it was me.

I pushed Attie's arm away, went to my aunt, and accepted the sack.

Then I waited, eyes to the sky. No lightning bolt struck me. No hand of God reached from the roiling clouds to smite me.

Glancing at Attie, I pulled out a loaf of bread and started tearing it apart to share.

CHAPTER TWENTY-FIVE

*I*n a stupor born of hunger, I crouched by a drift log and submitted to the mesmerizing spell of the breakers rushing the mouth of the creek, pulling out again, rolling the fist-sized rocks against each other in an odd, low roar.

Overhead, gulls rode the stiff wind and scolded me with their squalling. They knew, it seemed, they'd have to fight me for the smallest bite of anything edible that might wash up.

This was the end. This rocky, rank-smelling beach was our Eden. What a comfort, I thought, to know that these waves had been crashing on these rocks since time began, and the universe would not have cared if the next one rose up and simply swept us all away like so much wreckage.

After leaving the Bray ranch, we had dragged ourselves up the shoreline three or four miles until finally, at this bleak spot, we found ourselves unable to take one more step. Behind us pressed the dark, forbidding forest full of wild beasts. To the west, the pounding ocean. Between them we'd clung for three days now, without shelter or any bite of food since my aunt's bread.

I slapped my arms for warmth and looked around at the others. Attie was trying to fan wet driftwood into flame. Mollie cradled the listless Ruthie, who had long since given up crying. Nell sat weeping and mumbling to herself.

God help us.

Yes, I was envisioning the real God again. My God, anyway. God as I'd imagined Him before Joshua filled my mind with visions of *him* as God. No more chanting, no more hypnotic repetition. Now I was just offering up a simple, heartfelt prayer.

Please, God, help us.

A receding wave revealed a dead crab. With a primitive surge of renewed strength, I scrambled up and stumbled toward it over the loose, slippery rocks.

"Mine," I muttered at the seagull who got there first. In a fury I flailed as it rose, wings flapping around my head. Desperate, I swatted the crab from its beak and snatched it up.

I tore that crab apart like some ravenous savage, cutting my fingers on the sharp shell as I dug out the meaty bits and stuffed them in my mouth. Then I stopped, gagging as the putrid taste registered. Falling to my knees in the waves, I retched again and again, the foul stuff falling into the foam, blowing into my tangled hair.

At last I felt Attie pulling me up.

"'And the sea gave up the dead which were in it,'" she intoned, "'and death and hell delivered up the dead which were in them....'"

Her voice sounded so strange. Slowly I straightened, and with a creeping trepidation turned to look up at her.

Her eyes! Blank. Hollow. These were eyes, I saw, that must gaze on fantastic scenes—spirits and beings of another world. What hellish visions, I couldn't know.

"Oh, Attie," I said, and tenderly wrapped her in my arms.

She stayed stiff for an instant, then collapsed against me, clinging.

I have always felt my simple prayer was heard and answered, for the next day we were found by an ordinary man.

As he thrashed his way out of the forest's thick undergrowth of sword fern and salal, Attie stood, breathless, staring as if waiting for him to announce himself as Joshua.

Instead, astonished, he dropped his bush hook to his side and said, "What in the Sam Hill are you girls doing here?"

Attie's face fell. Obviously there was nothing of the spirit about him. He was simply a timber inspector who'd been following the creek and chanced upon our wretched little camp.

Attie drew a deep, weary breath, then let it out. "We're members of the Bride of Christ Church."

The man's eyes widened. "That Creffield bunch?"

Attie nodded. "He's gone to prepare a place for us. A new home in the Queen Charlotte Islands. Then he'll come fetch us."

"But —"

"In the meantime, we've been commanded to stay."

He regarded his own boots for a moment, then looked up. "I see you ladies haven't heard then. He's dead. Somebody shot him down. 'Bout a week ago."

Attie gave a strange laugh and, oh, it hurt me to see her grasping for some shred of dignity. "Yes, we've heard that's what they're saying, but it's not true. You see, he's going to rise again."

"Attie," I said, "the resurrection was supposed to be in three days. If he was shot a week ago —"

She gazed out to sea. "He told me it would be the first Sunday." She turned to the man. "What day is it today?"

"Well, Saturday."

"There!" she said. "You see!"

I sighed. I saw nothing but my cousin's incredibly stubborn faith, the faith I used to admire, the faith I'd wished I had. Now I saw it was a faith that had completely blinded her.

The man scratched his head. "So, how long you been here?"

"Three weeks?" Nell answered, lowering the wet,

frayed blanket she'd been struggling to make serve as a shelter. "Three days? Sir, perhaps you could help me to secure this tent." How strange she sounded. How detached. As if we were ladies on a lovely outing only slightly vexed at the wind, as opposed to a handful of desperate souls very near perishing.

The man took a deep breath. "Forgive my saying it, but you're not any of you looking too good, and with the baby there . . . I think we'd better figure out how to get you out of here."

Attie gave him the fiercest look. "Romans eight-eighteen. 'For I reckon that the sufferings of this present time are not worthy to be compared with the glory which shall be revealed to us.'"

"Joshua's dead, Attie," I said gently. "And he's not coming back."

Everyone stared at me. But I knew it was true now. In saying it aloud, I was finally admitting it to myself.

I closed my eyes. "It's over."

A long silence, with only the roar of the ocean tumbling the rocks.

Then the man coughed, genuinely grieved, it seemed, at our pathetic dilemma. "Let me give you what I can here," he said, and opened his rucksack to hand out sea biscuits and powdered milk.

I stumbled to his side. Mollie joined me, and then Aunt Nell.

Only Attie stood away, her back turned.

The next day, a different man appeared at our camp, saying my father, having received word of our plight from the kindly timber inspector the day before, had arranged for him to guide us back.

"My father sent you?" I said in wonderment. "Are you sure you mean *my* father?"

"Well, he said his was the youngest of the bunch. You are Vic Hurt's girl, aren't you?"

I nodded, my throat tightening. To think I might still claim this title.

"He's the one. Had to go see to your sister in Seattle or he'd have come himself. You'll have to make the trek around the cape on foot, but he's hired you all a wagon, waiting at Oceanview."

I rose slowly, unsteadily.

I didn't look to the others, who remained huddled against a drift log.

"Attie?" I said. "I'm sorry. I'm going."

She didn't speak. She didn't meet anyone's eyes. She merely picked up her bundle and stood, head bowed, as if waiting to be directed.

CHAPTER TWENTY-SIX

*A*fter our long wagon ride home on the rough, Alsea mountain road, Mama fed me, fussed over me, and put me straight to my own soft bed.

It was to be a long time before I slept easily, though, before I stopped tossing and turning with the sense of something urgent left undone, the feeling that Joshua was watching me still. Every time I woke from an end-of-the-world nightmare, on fire with fear, I had to find my place again, remind myself: *Joshua's dead. He's not coming back. You don't have to be afraid anymore.*

In Seattle, Maud was quite bizarre in her grief, Papa said, showing no emotion when Joshua was buried, calmly claiming he was not truly dead but would rise again. Then, three days later, in police detention as a witness, she exploded into hysterics, her cries like those of a wild animal as she pleaded to be taken to the cemetery to await Joshua's resurrection, insisting that were she not there, like Mary Magdalene at Christ's tomb, Joshua would declare her unfaithful and her soul would be lost for all eternity.

Esther too, having joined Maud in Seattle, staunchly claimed to await this resurrection.

In a way, I understood. Not that I expected Joshua to rise. But my sister and Esther had been his closest, most faithful followers. They were truly his Chosen Ones. And if faithfulness to him was not to be rewarded, it would surely be punished, with those who clung the longest the most reviled. No wonder they couldn't bear to let go.

During George Mitchell's trial, Mama and I stayed home in Corvallis while Papa looked after Maud and Esther in Seattle and, along with many other men from Corvallis, testified in George Mitchell's defense.

While it was George Mitchell who was charged with murder, it was Joshua they were compelled to discuss, Joshua who dominated the trial, even from the grave. Every miserable, twisted bit of our sect's history was revealed for public inspection as one impassioned group of men—the fathers and brothers and husbands—desperately tried to make another group—the jury—grasp the mysterious and awesome power over women this man possessed. What if these had been *their* women? Wouldn't *they* have run for *their* guns?

No one tried to pretend for one minute George Mitchell hadn't shot Joshua, and Maud was asked to tell the story again and again, how they had walked down the hill from their rooming house right before it happened. Joshua had promised to buy her a new skirt, she said, a sad little revelation, almost as pathetic to me as the part about the shot ringing out just as she stepped on the drugstore's penny scale.

Women attending the proceedings made a hero of the handsome young George Mitchell, showering him with flowers as he was escorted out each day, thronging the King County courthouse halls, clamoring for his attention. I had no difficulty imagining this scene, the glowing looks on their faces as they pressed closer, reaching out to touch him.

Strangely, no one batted an eye when George declared that God Himself had directed him to deliver up the spirit of Joshua Creffield. Apparently personal communications from the Almighty were perfectly acceptable provided God's message was one the majority could so heartily approve.

So it hardly came as a surprise when the twelve men of the jury required little more than an hour to declare George Mitchell not guilty. In truth, he wasn't the one on trial: Joshua was. And Joshua had been found guilty. George Mitchell had simply done the world a favor by exacting the penalty *before* a trial. For everyone agreed and seemed to consider themselves quite rational in believing this: The price for commanding the love and loyalty of other men's women is death.

Papa had only been home from Seattle a day or two when he appeared at the back kitchen door in the middle of the afternoon, startling Mama and me.

"Why, Vic," Mama said. "What are you doing home

at this hour? You're not looking for supper early, are you, because I haven't got — "

"Sarah."

Mama stopped. She set down her rolling pin. I saw in my father's face some blackness yawning before us.

"It's Esther," he said. "Esther Mitchell's shot her brother."

My knees gave way. I caught myself on the edge of the table. It's never going to end, I remember thinking. Never.

"It just came in over the wires," Papa said, helping me to a chair. "Walked right up to George in the Seattle train station and put a gun to his head."

"God in Heaven." Mama's hand pressed her breast. "Is he — "

Papa nodded. "Dead."

He stood there, hunched with the weight of it all.

"There's more, I'm afraid."

More?

"They're saying it was Maud who gave her the gun."

THE CORVALLIS TIMES

July 20, 1906

QUOTE FROM THE DISTRICT ATTORNEY WHO PROSECUTED CREFFIELD IN PORTLAND, SEPTEMBER 1904:

"George Mitchell went up to Seattle and killed Creffield, who should have been killed, as any other decent man anywhere would have killed him. He did it for his sisters. Now this girl shoots him down as he is ready to start home. My opinion is that no girl who is not utterly depraved could do such a thing, especially in view of what her brother did for her.

"Mitchell was a nice, steady young fellow and I am very sorry to learn of his death. I believe that Maud Hurt Creffield ought to be punished just as severely as Esther Mitchell, for Mrs. Creffield put the girl up to shooting her brother."

When Mr. Manning was seen this morning, a rumor was being circulated on the street that Esther Mitchell had committed suicide.

"It's a good thing," he said when he heard it. "Mrs. Creffield ought also to commit suicide."

CHAPTER TWENTY-SEVEN

The rumor about Esther committing suicide wasn't true.

What *was* true, though, was that Maud and Esther didn't care whether they lived or died.

Maud stopped eating.

"I'm prepared to hang for murder," Esther declared, refusing to plead insanity.

Maud followed suit, declining to lay claim to any excuse of mental illness, even though Papa begged her to do so and hired good lawyers.

Esther was brought to trial first and ultimately found not guilty by reason of unsound mind. Maud too was declared insane, even before her trial, but the district attorney appealed the ruling. He wanted both of them deemed sane. Only sane women could be tried and hanged for murder, and that's what he hoped to do. So Maud and Esther stayed locked in jail.

The record-breaking heat and forest-fire smoke of that awful summer gave way to the rains of autumn, and still the legalities dragged on.

My parents visited Maud in November and came home reporting her spirits were abysmally low. Determined to refuse all food, she was wasting away on purpose. The jail matron reported she had dropped an incredible seventy-five pounds. Worst of all, she still claimed faith in Joshua.

"She says if she dies," Papa told me, "she wants to be buried at his side."

All that week it rained and stormed far and wide, and the rivers flooded the land. Trees fell; bridges were washed out. Roads were impassable and trains delayed.

And then, Saturday morning, the telegram arrived.

Maud was dead.

Joshua still reached for us, even from the grave.

The Bonney-Watson funeral parlor was set on a corner just a few steep blocks from our Seattle hotel. It was Monday afternoon when my father and I entered the vestibule. Clutching his arm, I looked into the chapel.

Up front, Maud's coffin; in the dim light, her profile.

My breath stopped.

Dead. My sister was dead.

Papa steadied me. Oh, I felt sick. How I wanted it all over with. The train trip had been so long and grueling. We two had come up from Oregon alone, my poor mother having fallen into a grief so profound, she could not bear the stress and exhaustion of another journey.

Every mile, every framed view out our rain-streaked window had been nothing but flooded land and broken trees. Wreckage. The end of the world.

And now this.

Did the memories of such terrible things ever recede into the past? Did I dare console myself with that hope?

Frank and Mollie arrived. We greeted each other and took seats in front, our backs to the emptiness of all the unfilled pews. So pitiful, so bleak. Why hadn't I thought to bring flowers? For there was only one limp bouquet on the coffin, no doubt provided by the undertakers themselves.

Just as one of those gray men got up to speak, there was a rustling behind us and we turned.

Esther, escorted by two men. For the funeral, she'd been allowed out of jail.

I hardly recognized her, so great was the change, so ravaged was she by her months in the jail cell. Shadows haunted her dark eyes; her delicate hands trembled.

Oh, Esther. Esther with the beautiful golden hair. Was it possible I'd once imagined this wretched creature knew and understood everything I did not? Was it true that in what seemed some dim past, I had envied her for being, along with Maud, Joshua's Chosen?

For at this moment, with my sister in her coffin and Esther looking ready for the grave herself, I saw clearly that what had once so sorely grieved me — being second best in Joshua's eyes—could only be counted now as my blessed deliverance.

Papa stood and made a place for Esther between himself and Frank.

The service was brief and grim. No music. I hardly heard what was said, for in my mind's eye I was envisioning my sister as she'd been before her fall—strong and beautiful, sure of herself and confident in her faith. At the end, as we filed forward to take our final farewells, it was Esther who broke down, crying and throwing herself against the coffin, reaching in to caress Maud's pale, waxy cheek.

Only Papa and I rode in the carriage with Maud's coffin to the hilltop cemetery.

He held a black umbrella over me as we approached the pit where we would be leaving her. Standing there in the rain, I refused to glance at the grave to the left of hers.

Blinking tears, I spoke through clenched teeth. "I wish we didn't have to put her next to him."

"I know," Papa whispered, loosening my grip on his forearm to put his arm all the way around me. "But it's what she wanted."

Into the darkness they lowered her coffin, and the first clods dropped with soggy splats on the wooden lid.

I knew we wouldn't ever talk about Maud dying by her own hand. Papa would want to believe she'd simply died of a broken heart. Never mind that she had repeatedly declared she had nothing to live for. Never mind that she'd spoken of her own death with apparent knowledge of its imminence. Never mind that the following day, the coroner would report his findings: strychnine poisoning.

I bit my lip and looked out over the steely gray lake in the distance. Who could have imagined? When I followed my sister across the bridge into town that day to Bible study, I surely never dreamed the end would be this: Papa and me, standing at her grave.

CHAPTER TWENTY-EIGHT

𝒮eptember 1909

We live by the sea now, which seems to suit us.

Papa bought some forty acres at Waldport that year we left Corvallis, and others of us came too. Our story is known here, but not held too much against us. Newcomers are needed. New blood for new families.

I try to think of myself as a new person in all ways. I go by Mae now, not Eva, and intend to do so for the rest of my life.

I count myself fortunate to be the bride of Frank Johnson, a steady Swede from Minnesota. We have our own farm down at Oceanview, just eight miles from my parents.

Esther reappeared on Mama and Papa's doorstep in Waldport last spring, having been released from the asylum at Steilacoom on the promise she'd leave the state of Washington and return to Oregon. My parents took her in, of course, and now she drifts through their house like some sad ghost. I contrive never to be alone with her, and pretend not to hear the hymn she favors humming—"The Voice That Breathed O'er Eden." It's like a whisper from the grave.

We don't talk about Joshua. The closest Mama came once was saying that the whole Bride of Christ time seemed to her like a bad dream, best forgotten. I knew in her heart she couldn't have put it behind her so completely, though. After all, we lost Maud. You don't forget a thing like that.

During these fine September days when my chores are done, I sometimes wrap up in my shawl and walk along the road that runs by the rocky shore and down to the beach. I love the roar of the surf, the bracing salt air, and the gulls wheeling overhead.

But as I walk, the best of it is this: The flutterings of the baby I'm now carrying beneath my heart.

Frank painted the trim on our shingled cottage a cheerful red for me, and by next summer the pioneer rose I planted ought to be climbing right up over the front door. When the weather's pleasant, I plan to put the rocker out there on the porch.

Oh, and just think what bliss that will be—to sit rocking our baby, looking out over the wide blue ocean, dreaming of all the days we have still ahead of us.

In this world without end.

Amen.

Eva Mae Hurt

$\mathcal{I}$n researching this true story, I feel I've been walking among ghosts. My family's own farm lies on the Mary's River just south of Corvallis, and I pass the site of the Hurts' house — no longer standing — as I drive into town over Mary's River bridge every day.

My grandfather owned a small cottage on the coast situated precisely where the girls would have climbed up from the long stretch of beach to traverse the rocky shelf just north of Yachats (YA-HOTS), the new name given to Oceanview. I grew up spending summer weekends there, playing in nearby Starr Creek, named for Sarah Starr Hurt's family, some of the first white settlers in the area.

During college I worked two summers at the Cape Perpetua Visitors Center, driving that high and twisty road from Yachats around the cape each day, living in a little rented cabin, just across an open field from the hillside cemetery that contains Eva Mae's grave.

The impact of Franz Edmund Creffield's ministry

on the town of Corvallis, Oregon, was well documented in newspaper articles between the years 1903 and 1906. In recreating the story, I've relied mainly on these original accounts, since most of the official records and trial transcripts are mysteriously missing, the files apparently having been purged at some point. I've avoided the multitude of accounts written in later years, which often seem to repeat and pass on careless errors.

No matter how amazing a true story might be, facts strung together do not make a readable novel. Therefore I've taken the liberty of condensing some of the comings and goings of characters to streamline the narrative. Also, for the sake of clarity, certain people who were present during many of the scenes depicted are not mentioned by name. In no case, however, have I deliberately contradicted the known facts, and in all cases the main events of the story took place when and where I set them, at least to the extent this can be determined.

While much about the characters and their personalities is imagined, many of the smallest details are true: Eva Mae winning a prize for selling *The War Cry*, Sophie destroying her graduation dress, Maud stepping on a penny scale just as the fatal shot rang out. Also accurate is the timing of the San Francisco earthquake.

I feel it should be noted that although all the wives involved bore babies by their husbands, either during the time period of this novel or subsequently, there is no indication anyone had a child by Creffield.

After leaving Corvallis, many of the people involved in the so-called Bride of Christ Church, including the Hurts, settled on the Oregon coast. There Mr. Hurt sold real estate, involved himself in various business enterprises, and served as a commissioner of Lincoln County.

Sophie Hartley, interestingly enough, married Perry Mitchell, Esther Mitchell's remaining brother. They ran a little general store in Yachats, and Sophie served almost thirty-three years there as the post-mistress. She is buried in the Yachats Cemetery between her husband and her parents, Lewis and Cora, who divorced but ultimately remarried.

Attie Bray married a man who had been involved with Creffield's group early on. They lived on the banks of the Yachats River and raised two children.

In 1920, Frank and Mollie were living in the Tidewater area of the Alsea River with their five children when Frank came to an untimely end, killed by his own gun in what was officially written up as a hunting accident.

Esther Mitchell remained with the Hurts for several years until she became the third wife of James Berry, the man who had once been engaged to Maud and later testified on behalf of George Mitchell at his trial in Seattle. After only five months of marriage,

Esther poisoned herself with strychnine.

Mr. Berry, who was apparently an alcoholic and abusive husband, went on to marry Esther's sister, Donna Mitchell Starr (called Nell in the novel), who was divorced from Burgess (Bert) Starr after the trials. When this marriage also ended in divorce, Berry married Mollie Hurt, Frank's widow, almost as if determined to work his way down the list of Creffield's devotees.

In the end, however, Mollie was buried next to her first husband, with a headstone that reads, "Mollie, wife of Frank Hurt."

Their oldest daughter, Ruth, the baby carried by the girls in their trek around Cape Perpetua, was the last living character in this story. She died in Waldport on April 16, 1999.

Eva Mae's husband, Frank Johnson, was a farmer who also drove the stage, ran a hotel, and once used his team of horses to rescue two men from drowning at the ford of the Yachats River. He and Eva Mae had two sons and three daughters.

Eva Mae became a member of the Presbyterian Church. She lived to be ninety-four, and when she died in 1980, she was survived by three of her children, plus eight grandchildren, nineteen great-grandchildren, and fourteen great-great grandchildren.

The thoughts and feelings of Eva Mae Hurt as a young girl are, of course, the product of my imagination.

It has been my goal and is now my hope, however, that within this fictional framework, *Brides of Eden* contains the truth.

Corvallis, Oregon

March 2000

ACKNOWLEDGMENTS

Thanks to Rick Borstein, Marlene McDonald, Theresa McCracken, and Robert Blodgett for the generous sharing of research materials.

Thanks to the staffs of various libraries and museums including Mary Swanson at Oregon State University's Valley Library; Mary Gallagher and Judy Juntunen at the Benton County Historical Museum; Steve Wyatt at the Oregon Coast Historical Museum; Elizabeth Neilson at the Oregon State University Archives; Will Harmon, Special Collections, the University of Oregon Library System; the staff of the Oregon Historical Society. Also Judy Rathbun and Derrol Hockett at the Newberg Friends Cemetery; the staff of Lake View Cemetery in Seattle; Sherry Steele at the Boys' and Girls' Aid Society of Oregon.

For reading and commenting on the manuscript at various stages of its development: Molly Gloss, Nancy Ashby, Mike Kinch, Lill Ahrens, Lynne Martin, and my brother, Bob Welch.

Others who helped along the way were Elizabeth Potter, Rosemary Nichol, Kanoa Kimbell, John Eberhardt, Julie Scott, and Rose Troxel.

Thanks to Shadowsmith Photographics and the Camera Corner, both in Corvallis, Oregon.

Thanks to my agent, Robin Rue, for faith in this project, and to my editor, Alix Reid, for her wise insights and gentle persuasion.

For friendship and unfailing moral support during the writing of this book: Virginia Euwer Wolff, Margaret Chang, Joan Bauer, and Theresa Nelson.

Continuing lifelong gratitude for support to one of my very best friends, my mother, Marolyn Welch.

Special thanks to my daughter, Mary Crew, for enduring various modeling sessions, and to my son William Crew for his patient help in explaining the mysteries of my computer system. Thanks to son Miles Crew for doing well in college and making the turning of his room into added office space seem like a safe bet!

And finally, thanks, as always, for everything, to my husband, Herb Crew.

PHOTOGRAPHS

page x
Corvallis from the water tower, ca. 1890 —
Oregon Historical Society
OrHi 24895

page 9
Mary's River bridge — Oregon State University Archives
Photo #596

page 10
Turn-of-the-century Corvallis house (Kerr House) —
Benton County Historical Society & Museum, Philomath, OR
1999-001.0046

page 42
Laundry line — Author

page 87
Willamette river ferry, Beach house rented by Frank Hurt —
Benton County Historical Society & Museum, Philomath, OR
1999-001.0048

page 96
Corvallis Gazette — Benton County Historical Society & Museum,
Philomath, OR
1999-001.0031

page 102
Benton County Courthouse, ca. 1905 —
Benton County Historical Society & Museum, Philomath, OR
1999-001.0047

page 116
Boys' and Girls' Aid Society, 1905 — Oregon Historical Society
CN 020823

page 128
Boys' and Girls' Aid Society, girls' dormitory —
Oregon Historical Society
CN 009259

page 141
Girl at the piano, ca. 1905 — Author's collection

page 145
Corvallis Congregational Church — Benton County Historical
Society & Museum, Philomath, OR
1984-015.0143

page 153
Church of the Good Samaritan, June 1906 —
Property of the Division of Special Collections &
University Archives
University of Oregon Library System
Further reproduction or citing requires permission from the
Division of Special Collections & University Archives

page 161
Train near Yaquina, 1904 — From the collection of Rose Troxel,
used by permission

page 178
Cape Perpetua — Benton County Historical Society & Museum,
Philomath, OR
1999-001.0034

page 192
Cummins Creek — Author

page 208
Maud's grave, Lake View Cemetery, Seattle — Author

page 211
Angel at the gate — Author

page 212
Eva Mae Hurt — Oregon Coast History Center
Image #440